A Mrs.

A QUESTION *of* DEVOTION

Mindy — Enjoy! Anita

ANITA KULINA

BRANDT STREET PRESS

A Question of Devotion

by Anita Kulina

© 2017 Anita Kulina

Published by
Brandt Street Press
5885 Bartlett Street
Pittsburgh, PA 15217
www.brandtstreetpress.com

ISBN: 978-0-9742607-6-1
Library of Congress Control Number: 2016915564

Book Design by
Mike Murray
Pearhouse Productions
Pittsburgh, PA
www.pearhouse.com

Cover Art by
Jamey Jackson
www.nyackartcollective.com/jamey-jackson

Printed in the United States of America

*For my family, whom I love
more than words can say*

1

Mrs. B chomped her toast. She tapped her stubby pencil on the table—tap tap tap. She couldn't figure out what 8 down was. She had half the letters and was a little ticked at herself.

The crossword came in the evening paper but she had gotten into the habit of doing the puzzle in the morning. She always got the quick crossword but this Chicago one vexed her on a good day, and today was not starting out to be a good day.

An hour before, when she got out of the shower, the red light was blinking on her answering machine. It was Myrtle Monaghan, one of her friends from

Burchfield's Senior Center, and it sounded like she might be crying.

"Can you meet me, Edwina, before you play cards this morning?" Myrtle seemed to choke on the last word. "I'll wait for you at the bench by the bus stop."

Now, Mrs. B set her pencil down and glanced at the clock. Eight fifteen. She looked down at the milky coffee in her cup. It was tepid but she didn't want to take the time to warm it. Myrtle could already be waiting on the bench across from the church.

Taking a last bite of toast, Mrs. B pulled on a heavy blue sweater and dug through her purse. With the key she finally found under a handkerchief, she unlocked the deadbolt her daughter Helen had insisted on buying the last time she visited, and opened her front door.

Mrs. B paused for a second in the doorway, taking in the new day. It was cool. Crisp. She pulled a square red scarf from the sweater's pocket—a babushka, they called it back on Polish Hill, where she had grown up—and folded it into a triangle. Slowly, as she held the railing, she went down the five steps from the porch.

At the bottom of the steps she paused to put the babushka on her head. As she tied it under her chin she could hear the skritch skritch of Jimmy's broom. "Morning, Jimmy," she said.

"Morning, Ed!" Next door, Jimmy was sweeping his already-clean sidewalk. Though he was almost as old as Mrs. B, Jimmy never came down to the Senior Center. "No time," he told her once. "Always something needs done."

Jimmy had never married, but his house was always immaculate. Mrs. B was afraid to drop a crumb in his living room on the rare afternoons when his sister visited him and Mrs. B was invited for coffee.

"Isn't it a fine day?" he said, not looking up from his broom. "A fine day."

She nodded as she headed down the street toward the avenue. The gray sidewalk was cracked two doors down where a tree had grown too big, and Mrs. B stepped carefully to avoid tripping over the rise in the pavement.

Myrtle never called her on the phone. Whatever it was, it must be important.

Mrs. B passed the Roarke's, the Farrell's. Mrs. Papp was getting the paper from her front stoop. Across the street, Betty Daley was leaning out her window, shooing a pigeon off the roof of her porch.

"Morning, Mrs. B."

Mrs. B waved as a teenager ran past her in a school uniform. It looked like it might be Julie Kennedy, but Mrs. B wasn't sure. All those high school girls wore their hair so much alike, and with a uniform it was hard to tell. The girl ran toward the church. Probably late for Mass. The nuns sent the seniors at St. Mary's High School to Mass on Fridays instead of religion class.

At the corner, Mrs. B turned to her right and crossed the street. Across the avenue, on either side of the school building, stood the bare skeletons of booths waiting to be decorated for St. Mary's fall festival. When Mrs. B was a young mother, she'd taken her turn volunteering for the fair, sorting items for the New To You sale in the church basement, twisting crepe paper and hanging it along shelving while the school custodian tacked lights to the top of a booth. She was glad she didn't have to do that anymore. It raised a lot of money for St. Mary's, but it was a lot of work.

Making a sign of the cross as she passed the church, Mrs. B headed toward the bus stop. Myrtle was already sitting there.

"Are you okay?" Mrs. B sat down next to her friend.

Myrtle nodded and started to cry at the same time. No sobs, just big tears rolling down her ruddy face. Mrs. B reached into her purse and handed Myrtle a handkerchief, the embroidered one her cousin Minnie had given her for her birthday years ago. It had orange leaves on it and yellow flowers.

Mrs. B looked around. She didn't want Myrtle to be embarrassed, and she was glad they weren't in sight of the Senior Center door. Though in truth, half their friends couldn't see this far anyway.

She looked in the other direction toward the schoolyard. Empty. No one was around except for two people at the bus stop across the street. Neither of them paid the old ladies any attention.

Mrs. B opened her mouth to ask her friend what was wrong, then closed it again. When Myrtle wanted to tell her, she'd tell her. Instead, she reached out and held her friend's hand.

They sat quietly for a while, staring straight ahead at the church and school.

Both of Mrs. B's kids had gone to St. Mary's. The welcoming yellow-brick buildings were the reason she and Albert had moved to this part of the city. Their neighbors were welcoming, too, and the young couple soon felt right at home. Mrs. B's son Leo and Myrtle's son Ronnie were best friends in Little League, along with a little boy from around the block, Danny McCoy. Danny was the only one who had any athletic talent, but the three of them seemed to be experts on how to have fun. Even when they were getting into mischief, the antics of that trio could warm a heart of stone.

Maybe something was the matter with one of Myrtle's kids. Maybe that's why Myrtle was crying. Maybe not. Maybe Mrs. B just thought that because she worried about her own kids.

Mrs. B looked over at her friend. Myrtle was wiping her eyes with the handkerchief. Mrs. B patted her hand.

The two ladies watched the people across the street board the 85 bus. Then they watched Father Clancy leave the priest's house and get into his Cadillac.

Father always drove nice cars, and he wasn't fussy about them. When he was a brand new parish priest, he took the boys in the neighborhood fishing during the summer. He would let those raucous children crawl all over his car's nice upholstery.

Myrtle and Mrs. B loved Father Clancy. Most everyone in the parish did, right from the start. Leo, Ronnie and Danny were so excited the first time Father took them fishing all the way out at Pymatuning Lake. They could hardly sit still while they waited on Mrs. B's front steps for him to come by to pick them up. Then again, she had to admit, the three of them seemed just as excited when Father took them a mile down the hill to fish in the Monongahela River.

Leo would come back from fishing smelling of river water, even after she told him never to swim there. She'd scold the lot of them, but she couldn't stay mad because they were so happy. Leo and Danny and Ronnie would bounce through her back door, laughing and shouting and shoving each other. If Albert was working the night shift at the mill, he would be home on those hot summer afternoons. After he'd hollered at the boys for causing a ruckus, he'd sit them down at the kitchen table to hear their stories while they all ate crackers and Polish sausage and pickles and whatever cheese Mrs. B had in the house for Albert's lunch.

Myrtle watched Father drive away. Mrs. B followed her gaze. After another minute or two, Myrtle let go of Mrs. B's hand. She braced herself on the bench with her right arm, then stood up. "I better head home," she said. "Thank you, Edwina. You're a good friend."

So Myrtle didn't want to talk after all. What she wanted was comfort. "Aren't you coming to the Senior Center?" Mrs. B asked.

"I want to go home first and wash my face. I'll be down." Myrtle looked at the handkerchief. Mrs. B nodded. Myrtle handed the handkerchief back to her friend, then began to walk up the little hill to her house.

2

Mrs. B watched her friend until she disappeared from view. Then she looked at her watch. Her card game would start in ten minutes. She could still make it.

Poor Myrtle. Mrs. B hoped she was all right.

She crossed at the corner and went down the little hill that led to the Senior Center in the basement of St. Mary's Church. As she reached the door, she shifted her purse to her left hand so she could grab the doorknob with her right. A larger hand moved hers aside.

"Let me get that for you, Mrs. B."

Father Sean Flaherty was as young as Father Clancy was old. He was handsome and pleasant and eager and, in Mrs. B's opinion, a little too good to be true. She stepped aside and accepted his offer, stepping carefully over the doorstep with Father following patiently behind her.

"It looks like it's going to be a lovely day, Mrs. B, doesn't it? And I hear we have fish fingers on the menu for lunch."

What did he mean *we*? She didn't like that royal we. It reminded her of nurses and hospitals and things she'd sooner not think about. In an attempt to be polite, she forced a little smile.

Mrs. B didn't like Father Sean. He wore an earring. He did have a lovely Irish brogue, and he was always perfectly nice to her, but she had trouble getting past his earring, and the fact that he asked everyone to call him by his first name. She preferred her priests to be like Father Clancy. Father Clancy was an old-fashioned priest. Father Clancy had the good grace to be grumbly once in a while.

One of the men from the Senior Center walked over to Father Sean and started talking to him about money Father wanted to raise for an Irish organization. Father pulled him aside and Mrs. B made her way toward the coffee urn, stopping to set her purse on a chair at the card table on her way.

She shook some creamer into a blue mug, then filled it almost to the brim. Taking a spoon from a handful of mismatched silverware in a yellow mug, she gave the brew a little stir and carried it to the card table. From the corner of her eye, she could see Vic Mathews approaching.

Mrs. B hung her sweater on the back of her chair and sat down. She took the pinochle deck from the center of the table, snapped off the rubber band and began to shuffle the cards. Vic took a seat and then got up again and came back with a little tablet and a pencil just as Don Cermiani reached the table. Don wore a blue ball cap that said United Steelworkers on the front in white letters.

"Ed."

She nodded toward him. "Don."

He sat down to Mrs. B's right with his coffee, then blew on it and took a sip. Vic got up again and got a cup of coffee. Old Mike Rafferty pulled out the chair across from her.

"Morning, Ed."

"Morning, Mike."

She didn't look up until she'd finished shuffling. She set the cards in front of Don. He cut them and set them in front of her again. She began to deal. Because of the way they were sitting, it looked like she would be partners with Mike. She was glad. Yesterday she had partnered with Vic and he bid too high without the meld. Mrs. B secretly thought she and Don were the best players, but Don always seemed to have better luck.

Brushing her white bangs away from her eyes, she sat back and fanned her cards. A decent hand. Not great, but good.

People were still filtering into the Senior Center, mostly women headed toward the crafts table in the back of the room. No sign of Myrtle. Not yet, anyhow.

When her cards were all in order, she sat back to study the faces of each of the three men at the table.

Mrs. B didn't like any of these men. She didn't dislike them either, though it was tough sometimes not to. Vic could be surly and you had to watch so he didn't cheat, and Don was always double-checking her math when it was her turn to keep score. Don had been a laborer at the steel mill, and Mrs. B had been a bookkeeper. Which of them was likely to be better at math? And Don never took off that darn ball cap. Everyone knew he was bald. It wasn't like it was a secret.

But there was no one else at the Senior Center who played cards seriously. The women at the next table were playing 500 Rum. Mrs. B taught her kids to play 500 when they were in kindergarten. If she wanted a challenging game of cards she had to put up with Don's controlling attitude, Vic's constant complaining and salty language, and Old Mike.

Actually, when she thought about it, Old Mike was alright. Everyone called him Old Mike because he had a son, Young Mike, who was probably 65 now. Old Mike didn't talk much. He played cards well, so you knew he had a lot going on upstairs. Though he wasn't the best player at the table, he was good. A challenge. And Old Mike never ticked her off.

They played one hand. Without any of them speaking, Mike picked up the cards, shuffled, and handed them to Vic to cut just as Myrtle walked through the Senior Center door. Mrs. B caught her friend's eye and received a big smile and a wave. Mrs. B waved back as Myrtle headed toward a group of women at the crafts table. By the time Mrs. B picked up her cards, Myrtle was busily chattering away. She looked happy, almost giddy. What on earth was going on?

Mrs. B did her best to focus on the pinochle game. They played another hand, and only bickered once when Don was dealing and Vic thought he had dealt Mike one too many cards and shorted Vic. Which, to no one's surprise, turned out not to be the case. After the second hand they all got up, took a restroom break, got another cup of coffee—or in Old Mike's case, tea—and went back to the table.

Mrs. B stood behind her chair for a second, to see if she could see what Myrtle was doing, but from that vantage point all she could see was the back of Myrtle's head.

The deal and the rest of the game, as usual, were silent except for the bidding and an occasional exclamation or grunt if someone made an unexpected play. Vic tallied up the score and read it off. Then all four of them got up and walked toward the kitchen and then to the back of the room for lunch. The men headed toward long tables to the right. Mrs. B went to the left where the ladies congregated at little card tables, each with a centerpiece of plastic roses.

Sometimes I feel like a kid in a school cafeteria, Mrs. B thought as she made her way toward Anne, Myrtle and Rose, already sitting at one of the square tables toward the back of the room.

On her way, Mrs. B passed the mahjong ladies. Most of them spoke only Chinese, so they usually kept to themselves. Lily, who spoke English, waved her hand in greeting as Mrs. B passed. Mrs. B said "Nee how" to everyone, the way Lily taught her to years ago. Two of the ladies looked up and said, "Ni hao!" The others waved and smiled.

At the lunch table, Mrs. B's beige plastic tray made a comforting sound as it hit the tabletop. Myrtle looked good. Cheerful, even.

These three women were Mrs. B's closest friends at the Senior Center. She met Anne Barker when she and Albert first moved to Burchfield. Anne's cousin Mary owned the Burchfield Grill, where Mrs. B and Albert used to stop for fish sandwiches on Friday nights before the children were born. Anne had lived in Burchfield all her life and she seemed to be related, through blood or marriage, to half the people in the neighborhood. Glamorous by Burchfield standards, Anne had been a model in the days when artists drew clothing for newspaper ads. She still got her hair done every week at the beauty parlor, and her clothes were always the prettiest colors.

Myrtle Monaghan's curly hair was, as usual, sticking out all over the place from under her pink hair band. Myrtle was normally sweet and full of sunshine. She grew up in Burchfield, too, in the little house where she raised her own family and still lived now.

Rose O'Malley—little, quiet Rose—moved to Burchfield when she got married, just like Mrs. B did. A private person, Rose was. None of the other ladies at the table had ever even met her before she started coming to the Senior Center, though of course they would see her at Mass from time to time. Rose's husband was retired from the police force and her son was a detective. That was all they knew about her. Rose looked like she might be Italian, but Mrs. B wasn't even sure about that.

"We were talking about something on TV last night," Anne said as Mrs. B steadied herself on the table with one hand and pulled out her chair with the other.

"Did you watch channel 13? It was one of those nature specials," Myrtle said. Rose looked up and nodded at Mrs. B, then continued fussing with her macaroni and cheese.

"I was watching a movie," Mrs. B said.

"It was all about walruses. They're big, fat buggers," Myrtle said.

"I think my first husband was a walrus," Anne said. They all giggled.

The rest of the lunch was like any other of the numerous lunches they had shared together. Myrtle seemed perfectly fine. Why, Mrs. B thought. Why the sudden change?

3

It was three o'clock when Mrs. B left the Senior Center. The church fair would open in an hour or two. People were bustling around to get ready and little kids were already congregating around the bouncy castle. The very first booth at the end of the drive was the bake sale. Mrs. B walked toward it, stepping aside as someone hurried to drop off a pecan pie.

At the booth, she heard a curt "We're not open yet," and then the young woman looked up and apologized. "Oh, hi, Mrs. B. Sorry, we're so busy! I didn't realize it was you."

Mrs. B said, "I don't want to bother you, but I wonder if I can get a little something."

"We don't have the cash box out yet, but if you have exact change . . . "

Mrs. B fumbled through her change purse. Four dollar bills, two quarters and seven pennies. She had more than enough. "Can I have that little loaf of banana bread?" she asked.

When she got home, she pulled the mail out of the mailbox and picked up the evening paper from the porch. As she walked through the front door, out of the corner of her eye she saw a flash of color. A child's pink sweatshirt was lying across the seat of her glider.

She walked back outside, looked around, and then picked it up. Must have been a little girl on her way to the fair. She folded it gently, laid it back on the glider and went inside.

With a fresh pot of coffee brewing, Mrs. B cut herself a slice of banana bread, then cut the remainder of the loaf in two. She wrapped one half in plastic wrap and put it in the refrigerator and wrapped the other in aluminum foil and put it in the freezer. When the coffee was ready, she got out a cup and plate, spread some cream cheese on the banana bread, and sat down to read the paper.

On the second page, she saw why Myrtle had been crying.

Ron Monaghan, Myrtle's son, had been arrested. Money was missing from St. Mary's Church. A lot of money. More than Mrs. B would have thought the church had, until she remembered the large bequest from Dr. Harrigan last year. Or was that the year before?

Poor Myrtle.

Leo, Ron and Danny were friends all through grade school and even in high school, when Danny started to hang out with the athletes and Leo and Ron got in with a wilder crowd. From the day Danny's football scholarship took him to college, success followed that boy like he was riding the tail of a lucky star. In a million years, she wouldn't have guessed the kid with the muddy face, spilling milk at her kitchen table, would someday coach the Chicago Bears.

For Leo and Ron, though, things were different. They drifted from job to job, never caring if they were fired, or if they had a black eye, or if they woke up at a police station. Nothing seemed to interest the two of them except their nighttime carousing. Then one day—out of the blue, it seemed to Mrs. B—the two of them packed up Ron's old station wagon and left for California.

Something bad happened there. Mrs. B never knew what and she wasn't sure she wanted to know. Ron came back alone. The day he came home, Ron stopped at Mrs. B's house. He said he hadn't seen Leo for a while. He didn't even know where Leo was.

Mrs. B still didn't know.

But Ron, he'd been walking the straight and narrow for all these years now. At least that's what everyone thought. He was even on the board at St. Mary's Church. When they asked Ron to join, no one gave a lick about his past. Half the neighborhood boys were in trouble at some time or another. No, all the board cared about was the fact that Ron was a contractor. They were looking for someone to oversee work when the church needed repairs. For free, of course. Father Clancy asked Ron himself, and naturally Ron couldn't say no.

At the time, Mrs. B took Ron's position on the board as evidence of the turnaround in his life. Father Clancy once told Mrs. B that Ron had the second best attendance record at St. Mary's board meetings.

Walter Earnest, their treasurer, was first. Even though he was starting to get dementia, the date of a board meeting was one thing Walt never forgot.

No one had the heart to ask Walt to step down, so eventually Father Clancy started paying the bills for the church. They took Walt's name off the bank accounts and added Ron's last year, mainly because they needed two names and no one else on the board would take on the responsibility.

Mrs. B read to the end of the article. Ron had been released on bond and the trial date was pending.

Well then, why was Myrtle so cheerful this afternoon?

Before Mrs. B went to bed that night, she walked out to her front porch to see if the sweatshirt was still on the glider. It was gone. She looked down to the bottom of her street for a few minutes, watching the lights twinkling all around the fair.

4

Mrs. B pulled the knot to her babushka tight, then rattled the doorknob to make sure she had locked the front door. Chill air bit her cheeks. She was glad she wore her heavy jacket.

The whole time she was walking down to St. Mary's for Sunday Mass, she thought about the newspaper article on Ron Monaghan. She wondered if Father would mention it in his sermon. She didn't think he would but it was church business, and she was sure some people would want to hear all the lurid details.

Entering the center door of the church, she took off her gloves and dipped her fingers into the font to bless herself. Then she walked to the place where she always sat, a half-dozen rows from the back, and settled comfortably in the old wooden pew.

When Albert had worked the evening shift, they came to church together on Sunday mornings. And sat in this very row, she thought, running her palm tenderly along the handrail. When the kids were little they would sit between them, Helen next to her daddy, Leo next to his mama. Leo, bless his heart, would try with all his might to sit still. Eventually either Helen or Mrs. B would end up putting an arm around his shoulders to help him settle down.

When Mass started, Mrs. B sang the hymns quietly, going through the motions as she had done a million times before. After the gospel, Father Clancy went to the pulpit and started fussing with the microphone. Mrs. B sat back and kicked out the kneeler so she could use it as a footstool. Father looked tired. Or sad. Maybe he looked sad.

"Father Sean has been called away unexpectedly," he said, then coughed into the microphone. Pulling out a handkerchief, he resumed, " . . . for an indefinite period of time. His aunt has passed away, and he's gone back to County Cork to be with his mother. I'm sure we will all pray this week for his aunt's soul, and the souls of all the faithful departed."

He stuffed the handkerchief back in his pocket. "In happier news, our volunteers are counting the money raised Friday and Saturday during St. Mary's fall festival. The bake sale, as always, was a big success. The new t-shirt booth did well and, as usual, the chuck-a-luck wheel was busy all night. Those of you who stood in the long lines at the food concessions know the ham barbecue was well worth the wait.

"The church is grateful to Tom Bower from Bower Rentals for use of their castle bounce house.

"We don't know yet exactly how much money was raised, but we will list the final total in next week's bulletin, along with the name of the winner of the raffle for the basket of cheer.

"Now I know you're all waiting to hear who was victorious in the annual rivalry between the ladies' bingo in the church basement and the poker game next door in my garage. I hate to admit it, but bingo won again." Father Clancy grinned, but on his tired face it seemed a little forced. "We want to thank everyone who attended, and special thanks to all the hard-working volunteers who made it happen."

He paused and rubbed his nose, then made a sign of the cross. "Today's gospel was about gratitude. Jesus told us . . . "

Hmm, Mrs. B thought as she unzipped the top of her red quilted jacket. It certainly seemed convenient that Father Sean would disappear just when all that money went missing. She shook her head, then realized she had and wondered if anyone noticed.

She liked Ronnie Monaghan, but that didn't mean he wasn't a thief. The police didn't arrest him on a whim. And just because Father Sean wore an earring didn't mean he wasn't totally trustworthy. Mrs. B said a Hail Mary in penance for being uncharitable toward the young priest and went back to listening to Father's homily.

When he was done, Father Clancy fussed with the microphone again, then stepped down from the pulpit and headed back toward the altar. Mrs. B was relieved he hadn't mentioned Ron or the missing money.

When Mass was over, Mrs. B lifted herself from the pew as the organist started the recessional hymn. She turned and saw Myrtle a few pews beyond her, pulling pink gloves from her coat pocket. Mrs. B waited on the sidewalk for her friend catch up.

Myrtle put a glove on, then took it off and put it on the other hand, talking all the while. "Oh, Edwina, I'm glad I ran into you. I usually go to Saturday Mass but I didn't get there last night and then I didn't go to early Mass today because I, well, I just couldn't sleep and I didn't get up until nine o'clock. Nine o'clock! I can't remember the last time I slept that late but I couldn't sleep and I couldn't sleep and I tossed and turned so . . . "

She took a breath, then smiled. "Do you want to come up to the house and have some coffee cake? I made it last night and it turned out good."

Mrs. B said, "I would love some coffee cake."

The two women walked together to the corner and crossed the street to climb the little hill to Myrtle's place. It was a red brick row house. It must have been crowded when Myrtle and her husband were raising their three children, but now the little two-up-and-two-down was just the right size.

When she walked through Myrtle's front door, Mrs. B was surprised to see Ron in the living room, watching a soccer game. He looked up from the Sunday paper and said hello.

As the ladies sat down at the kitchen table, Ron turned the volume down on the television. Ron always was a polite boy. Even at his worst, he was always polite.

Myrtle started a pot of coffee. "Ronnie's come to stay with me until this awful mess is over." She dropped her voice low and leaned in toward Mrs. B.

"He didn't do it, you know. Ronnie. He didn't do what they said in the paper." She looked up. "You saw the paper."

Mrs. B nodded.

"Ronnie doesn't want Mary Beth and the kids to have to deal with all this. He's a good dad," Myrtle said. Mrs. B had seen Ron with Billy and Timmy, and agreed that he certainly seemed to be a good father. Though she didn't say so, Mrs. B had a suspicion that Ron was at Myrtle's because Mary Beth had become too hard to live with when the story hit the papers. It made her a little sad.

Myrtle went into the cupboard and got two round white cups and two white plates with pink roses. The coffee cake sat in the center of the kitchen table. Grabbing a butter knife from a drawer, she cut two pieces and handed one to Mrs. B. "Don't you love crumb topping? I love crumb topping."

5

An hour later, long after the ladies had finished the last bits of cake from their plates, the kitchen still smelled like cinnamon.

Mrs. B took another sip of the cooling coffee in front of her. Myrtle looked out the kitchen window for a few seconds, then turned toward Mrs. B. "This has been such a nice morning. I always like talking to you, Ed. I'm glad you're my friend."

Mrs. B was touched. "We've been friends a long time, Myrtle."

"No, not really friends," Myrtle said. "We knew each other because of the boys. But when I started going to the Senior Center, that's when we started to really be friends." She took their cake plates and put them in the sink. "I remember my first day there. You were the first person to come over and say hello to me."

Mrs. B hadn't thought about it, but she supposed she was.

Myrtle said, "I knew I'd know people there but I didn't want to go. Ronnie made me. And now look at us. What would we do without the Senior Center? It's like our little club."

Mrs. B knew that was true. "We're lucky to have a senior center in Burchfield. So many neighborhoods don't have one." She brushed some crumbs from the table and wadded them into her napkin. "My grandmother sat in her rocking chair, day after day after day. Whenever we came to visit, there she was, rocking."

"I know!" Myrtle exclaimed. "My grandma kept busy, but not the way we do. She was always scrubbing things that were already clean. She never had any fun." She leaned on the sink and turned to Mrs. B, a yellow sponge in her hand.

"We have fun, don't we? We have crafts class on Thursdays, and we can play cards if we want, and you always do. And bingo every other Tuesday, and we have our nice lunches every day and get to see all the ladies. And supper club sometimes, or they take us to a play, and we always get to go to a baseball game in the summertime. What would we do without the Senior Center?"

Myrtle squirted soap into a plastic basin and turned on the water. Mrs. B picked up a dishcloth and stood near the sink.

"We are a new breed of old people," Mrs. B said.

"Yes, we are. Happy old people," Myrtle said. "I like being an old lady. I never thought I would. I didn't know it would be fun."

Just then Ron spoke and they saw he was standing in the doorway, almost filling the little white doorframe. "Mom, I'm going down the avenue. You want anything?"

"Where are you going?" Myrtle said.

"Just down to play my number. I'll be right back."

"Okay, let me think . . . No, I got milk. I don't need anything."

He bent and kissed her. "See you in a few. Bye, Mrs. B."

Myrtle waited for the front door to close, then turned to Mrs. B. "You remember Friday morning, after I saw you, I came back to the house to wash my face? Well, Ronnie told me he didn't do it. He didn't steal that money. I told him, 'Well, Father didn't take it,' and he said, 'Mom, it's gone, but I didn't take it.'"

Mrs. B gave a little sigh. Kids don't always tell their parents the truth. Myrtle and Mrs. B both knew that. They had learned the hard way.

Still, there was Myrtle, smiling hopefully. "He didn't have his lying face. I could always tell when he was lying. Somebody else took that money and the police just think it's Ronnie. Now couldn't that be true?"

Though it seemed unlikely, Mrs. B admitted it was possible.

Myrtle turned on the faucet and rinsed a plate. "I bet we could find out where that money went. Me and you. Mostly you, really. You're so smart, everybody knows how smart you are. You went to college, and you read all those books all the time."

Mrs. B had to admit a part of her wanted to believe Ron. She said, "Secretarial college isn't the same as a regular college."

Myrtle was unfazed. "You're smarter than anyone at the Senior Center. You always know all the answers on Jeopardy."

Mrs. B dried the last plate and put it away. "Thank you for the coffee cake. I better get home. I'll see you tomorrow."

Myrtle turned to her, eyes filled with tears. "I don't want to go to the Senior Center tomorrow, Ed. People are going to talk about my Ronnie. They're going to say terrible things about him. They're going to say I'm a bad mother."

Mrs. B looked her straight in the eye, the dishcloth still in her hand. "Remember last year, when Alma Harrison's son robbed the bank downtown?"

Myrtle nodded, wiping her eyes with the end of her apron.

"Nobody said mean things," Mrs. B said. "We all felt sad for her."

Myrtle's face brightened. "All I felt was sad. 'Poor Alma,' that's what I thought."

"You come to the Senior Center tomorrow. It'll be fine. You'll see." Mrs. B folded the dishcloth and set it on the counter. She took her red jacket off the back of the kitchen chair and started to put it on. "Was that a new school picture of Billy on top of your TV?"

"Yes! Isn't he getting big!" Myrtle ran to get the photo.

6

At home, when Mrs. B climbed to the top step of her porch, she heard a timid "Hi."

A little girl in a pink sweatshirt was on her glider. Her feet barely touched the cement floor of the porch.

"Hello," Mrs. B said.

"I'm Kelly."

"How do you do, Kelly. I'm Mrs. B." She waited for a response, but Kelly just sat on the glider, swinging her legs and watching her pink tennis shoes as they went back and forth. Finally Mrs. B asked, "Can I do something for you?"

Kelly got up from the glider and pointed. "That's where I live. In Aunt Laverne's house."

Mrs. B remembered the afternoon, a week or so ago, when a little girl had waved to her from Laverne Grey's porch. There was a truck out front then, and a couple of young men were carrying a couch into the house while a too-thin brunette in a gold jacket animatedly directed them.

Laverne had told Mrs. B a couple of weeks before that she was moving to Florida and planned to rent the house to her young niece. Mrs. B hadn't known the woman well. Laverne was a little younger, and spent her time at the bar rather than the Senior Center, and she didn't go to their church. But they always said hello to each other and had been neighbors for twenty years.

Kelly spoke again. "Aunt Laverne told me you were a nice lady. She said if anything ever happened I should come over here."

Mrs. B was surprised at this, but she tried not to show it.

"Nobody's home at my house. My mom is supposed to be home from work now." She turned her face toward Mrs. B and said, "I can't watch myself. I'm only eight."

Hoping to mask her concern, Mrs. B put on a warm smile. "Well, don't you worry one bit." Unlocking her front door, she said, "Did you eat lunch yet?"

"No . . . "

"Well, let's go in and call your mother. Do you know her number at work?"

Kelly looked a little hopeful. "I know her cell phone number."

"Let's give her a call and I'll make something for us to eat."

Almost instantly, Kelly's face relaxed. She walked through the door ahead of Mrs. B and made a beeline for the kitchen. She stood in front of the refrigerator, then turned and asked, "Do you have anything to drink?"

"Yes, you can look and see what you'd like, but first let's call your mother." Mrs. B walked to the phone in the hallway. "What's her number?"

Kelly ran to the phone. "Here, I'll call her." She hit the big white buttons slowly and then waited.

"Mom, where are you?" A pause. "It's okay, Mrs. B across the street is watching me." Another pause. "No, the yellow house." Pause. "Okay, bye." She hung up the phone and turned to Mrs. B. "She said stay here until she gets here."

Mrs. B went to the refrigerator and pulled out a loaf of raisin bread and a package of American cheese. She took a frying pan from the bottom shelf in the cupboard and put a little margarine in it from a plastic tub on the kitchen table.

Kelly opened the refrigerator. "You don't have any pop."

Mrs. B got a juice glass from the china hutch in the corner of the kitchen. "Which do you like better, orange or grape?"

Kelly thought about it. "Orange."

Mrs. B poured a glass of orange juice and set it on the table. She made two cheese sandwiches and put them in the frying pan.

"You can set the table," she told Kelly.

"What?"

"Go in the cupboard and get two plates and put them on the table."

Kelly took two plates from the bottom shelf and set them down in a stack on the flowered plastic tablecloth.

"No, put each one in front of a chair."

Kelly separated them. Mrs. B flipped the sandwiches over.

"Now put a napkin next to each one, on the left."

Kelly took two napkins from a clear plastic holder, pulling out too many and stuffing the others back. "Oh, like at the diner!" She folded one in half, set it next to a plate and smoothed it, then went on to the other. Mrs. B poured herself a mug of cold coffee from the coffeemaker and put it in the microwave.

The phone rang just as Kelly was taking the last bite of her sandwich. "That's my mom!" The little girl ran and answered it before the second ring. "Mom?" She smiled. "The yellow one." She hung up and went into the living room and stood by the door. Mrs. B put the dishes in the sink and followed her.

A young brunette was standing outside. Her dark hair was caught up in a gold ponytail holder. Mrs. B opened the door.

"Mom!" Kelly ran to her.

The young woman looked down at Kelly quickly, then up at Mrs. B. "Hi, I'm Michele, Kelly's mom. Thanks for keeping an eye on her until I got home. I work at the casino. We don't always get out on time."

"I'm Mrs. B. Nice to meet you. Would you like to come in?" Mrs. B asked.

"Yeah, okay, for a minute." Michele plopped onto the barcalounger and stuck her legs straight out in front of her, as if she were exhausted.

Kelly wandered over to a little bookshelf on the other side of the room, turning around to say, "We ate grilled cheese sandwiches."

"That's nice," Michele said as she turned to Mrs. B. "My brother Anthony dropped her off. He was supposed to wait for me if I wasn't home. I guess he forgot I was at work."

Mrs. B didn't like to meddle in people's affairs, so she didn't say what she was thinking. Instead she said, "Kelly and I had a nice lunch together. She tells me she started school at St. Mary's."

"Aunt Laverne said that's where she should go." Michele looked around the room.

Mrs. B remembered her manners. "Would you like a cup of coffee?"

Kelly was at the bookshelf, pulling books out and looking at the covers, then putting them back. Michele looked at her daughter, then back at Mrs. B. "No, thanks, we have to get going. It was nice of you to watch her. I hope she wasn't any trouble."

"I enjoyed her company," Mrs. B said.

Kelly came over and squeezed next to her mother on the chair. "Mrs. B likes arithmetic too. When she was little that was her favorite subject, just like me."

Michele reached into what looked like a large, shiny tote bag but might have been a purse. She pulled out a comb and ran it through Kelly's hair, turning to Mrs. B as Kelly squirmed. "We need to get going. I have plans for later."

"Is Rocky coming over?" Kelly asked.

"No, I broke up with him."

Kelly shook her hair as Michele put the comb away. Mrs. B said she was sorry to hear that.

"Oh, it's okay, I have a date with a guy from work. I like him better anyhow." Michele turned to Kelly and said, "Where's your coat? We need to go home. I need to get ready."

"I didn't wear my coat. I wore my sweatshirt."

"Well, get your sweatshirt." She rose. "Thank you, Mrs. B. I appreciate it and Kelly does, too, don't you, Kelly?"

"Thanks, Mrs. B." As they were leaving, Kelly stopped in the doorway and looked up at her mother. "Who's going to watch me?"

"Come on!" Michele took her hand and pulled her through the door, talking to Kelly as they walked. "Who always watches you? Your cousin Julie."

Before Mrs. B locked the door, she heard Kelly's voice trailing off with, "I don't want Julie to watch me. All she does is talk to Patrick on the phone."

7

Mrs. B thought about her new neighbors as she waited for her turn at the computer. It had been a long while since a child sat at Mrs. B's kitchen table, and Mrs. B found it pleasant to spend time with little Kelly. What Mrs. B thought of the girl's mother, however, was still up for debate.

Don clicked, then cursed. "Click, double click, what's the difference," he muttered as he fumbled with the mouse.

Tony Cordonelli, who owned the little store next to the bank, had two boys. The younger one, Patrick, just started college and today he was teaching a computer class at the Senior Center. Mrs. B didn't know him well but she did see him sometimes with Julie Kennedy, who lived at the very top of Mrs. B's street. As young as Patrick was, Mrs. B thought he was a better teacher than the fellow who taught it last time.

There were two computers in the back of the Senior Center near the crafts table, and the seniors were allowed to use them any time they wanted. Mrs. B hadn't used a computer since she took the class last summer. She thought she might, if she knew why to use them at all. She had a typewriter at home, an electric one, so she didn't need a computer to write letters. This class was supposed to talk about the internet, though, and that intrigued her.

Patrick gave Don one of those patient looks teachers seem to cultivate. "One click does one thing, a double click does another. You have to learn both. You'll catch on in no time. Go ahead and give it another try."

Mrs. B was sure she could do it. She wondered if Patrick got bored hearing the same complaints. Everybody seemed to have trouble with that clicking thing.

When it was her turn, Mrs. B did remember and could click and double click. After a few times, she stepped aside for the next person.

Patrick had everyone sit back down and surprised them by saying, "Now let's forget about the computer for a few minutes. I want each of you to tell me what you do in your spare time. What interests you? It may sound strange, but it will help me to teach you."

He called on Don first. "My wife and I watch all the travel shows on TV. We want to go to Paris for our 50th anniversary."

Paris? At cards last week, Don said his son Gregory had stopped by with two bags of groceries. Not exactly a gift you bring parents who galavant all over creation, Mrs. B thought.

Anne said she liked keeping up with the latest fashions and talking to her friends. Old Mike surprised them all by saying he watched the cooking shows and sometimes tried out the recipes. When it was Mrs. B's turn, she said simply, "Current events."

Patrick asked Anne to come back up to the front of the class and have a seat at the computer. The rest of them gathered around.

Patrick called up a search engine and had Anne type the word *fashion*, then hit the enter button. A list came up. When he had her click on one of the items, a screen appeared that looked like the table of contents from a fashion magazine.

"Well, look at that!" Anne said.

"Now click on a picture," Patrick said. It took her to an article and groups of little photos. He asked her to click on everything she saw—"Just experiment. Make it fun!"—and as Anne looked at photos of dresses and jewelry, Patrick asked Don to sit at the next computer.

When it was Mrs. B's turn, she learned that the search engine had a *News* button at the top. When she pressed it, though, she was disappointed to see a list of lurid headlines, not at all what she liked to read.

Then Patrick told her to type *best news sites*. She did so, wondering how on earth the computer would know what she thought was best, and was happily surprised to find a list that better suited her. She followed Patrick's instructions and clicked on everything she saw, finding page after page of news.

Patrick showed them all how to click at the top of any page they didn't like, and they could make it disappear. That was fun, too.

Everyone was laughing and talking, looking over each other's shoulders and generally enjoying themselves until, before they knew it, it was four o'clock and Father was there to lock the doors to the church basement. As they gathered up their belongings and headed toward the exit, Mrs. B complimented Patrick on his teaching skills.

"It's a trick, really. A professor taught it to me. If I find out what someone likes, I can teach them to use the computer. I even taught Father Clancy. We started talking about football and he picked it right up."

My goodness. She didn't think of Father as the technology type, though she did remember seeing him early one morning in front of the bank, using the ATM machine. Mrs. B had never used it herself, and she had been impressed. And he even used a computer? We are never too old to learn.

As Mrs. B and her friends left the Senior Center, Anne said, "I smell French fries." They looked around and saw the back door to the Burchfield Grill was propped open.

"Must be hot in the kitchen," Mrs. B said.

"Now I'm hungry for French fries," Anne said.

"Oh, I'm out of milk!" Mrs. B said.

"Now how on earth did French fries remind you of milk?" Anne asked.

Mrs. B laughed. "I don't have any idea." She said goodbye to Anne and headed toward Tony's store.

As she rounded the corner, Mrs. B passed two young men standing in front of the Grill. "Hi, Mrs. B," said one as he tipped his cap.

Mrs. B said hello. She knew he was a boy who had played Little League with Leo, but she didn't remember his name. She liked the hat tip.

When she got to Tony's store, she saw Patrick had beaten her there and was already behind the counter, talking on his cell phone. Mrs. B nodded hello to him and he nodded back, still chatting with his friend about something. Sports, it sounded like.

She walked a little farther and perused the bright dairy case on her right. Milk, eggs, butter. I still have some butter, she thought, and I think I have three eggs. She took a quart of 2% milk from the case and carried it to the counter. Patrick rang her up, took her money, gave her change and put the milk in a plastic bag, all the while still talking to his friend on the phone.

These kids are tied to their cell phones, Mrs. B thought. They talk to people who are far away instead of the people right in front of them.

Mrs. B passed the bank and then the Grill on her way back. As she walked by, the two men outside opened the door and went in. She could see Vic at the bar, cursing and shaking his fist at the television. It looked like two other men were arguing in a booth. She wrinkled her nose at the stale beer smell.

She didn't see him in there, but she wondered if Ron Monaghan was drinking again.

8

By the time Mrs. B was halfway up her street, Kelly was on her way down to meet her.

"Hi, Mrs. B!"

"Hello, Kelly. How are you today?"

"Good." She fell in step with Mrs. B. "Julie's watching me but she's doing her homework and I said I wanted to go over Mrs. B's and she said okay. Can I come over?"

Mrs. B was a little tired and didn't like the idea of Kelly being out after dark, even though it wasn't yet five o'clock. She almost said no, then glanced at Kelly's upturned face and changed her mind. "Yes, you can come over."

They climbed her steps and Kelly picked up the newspaper while Mrs. B fished her front door key from the bottom of her purse. Mrs. B opened the door and Kelly flew in ahead of her. Taking off her coat, Mrs. B headed toward the kitchen with the milk and the afternoon paper. Kelly tossed her jacket on the loveseat and followed.

Mrs. B put the milk in the refrigerator. "Did you eat dinner yet?" she asked as she carefully lifted a covered enamel saucepan out of the refrigerator, using both hands to make sure it didn't spill. She set it on the stove and turned the burner on.

"No," Kelly said. "Mom's bringing chicken nuggets. She's coming home late. She told Julie somebody cashed a big check at the casino and they're buying everybody drinks."

Mrs. B took two small glasses from the china hutch and filled them with grape juice. She sat one in front of Kelly, who was standing by the kitchen table. Then she sat the other at her chair near the refrigerator and began to look at the front page of the paper. She was quickly absorbed in an article about a local musician who had been arrested in Ireland as part of an IRA splinter group, one of the little rebel factions that refused to give up the cause.

Kelly looked at her for a while, then headed toward the living room. She came back with a set of dominoes from the bottom of the bookcase.

"Is this a game?"

Mrs. B had just turned to the puzzle. She paused to consider, then set the paper aside. Maybe Kelly didn't get much attention at home. "Yes, that's a game. Would you like to play it?"

"Is it hard?" Kelly said. "I don't want to play if it's hard."

"You won't know until you try." Mrs. B cleared a space on the kitchen table between the two of them. They flipped the dominoes so they were all face down. Then they each picked one.

"I got a six, and you got a five," Mrs. B told her. "So I go first. Count out seven for each of us."

When Kelly was done, Mrs. B said, "Now put them up like this, so I can't see yours." Mrs. B stacked hers on their sides, with their backs toward Kelly. Kelly picked hers up one by one and carefully laid the rectangular tiles in a row.

Mrs. B pushed the rest of the dominoes to the side, then laid a double-six tile between them on the flowered plastic tablecloth. "Now do you have a six on one of yours?"

"Like this?" Kelly showed her a six-and-one. "Or this?" She showed her another, with three and three.

"Like that one," Mrs. B said, pointing to the first tile.

They played until the soup was warm. When dinner was ready, Mrs. B poured a bowl for herself and a little bowl for Kelly. "You don't have to eat it if you don't like it," she said as she placed it in front of her.

"What is it?"

"It's vegetable soup."

"What's in it?"

"Think about it," Mrs. B said. "What do you think is in it?"

"Vegetables."

Mrs. B handed her a teaspoon, then pulled out a loaf of rye bread. She buttered a piece, placed the knife on the table by the margarine and picked up the newspaper.

"What about the game?" Kelly asked.

"We can play after dinner." She turned to the crossword while Kelly stared at the soup, then picked up her spoon and tasted a tiny bit of the broth. She stirred it around for a while and found a carrot.

"I like carrots," she said.

"There's carrots and potatoes in there. I bet you like potatoes too."

"What's this stuff?"

"That's cabbage. You don't have to eat the cabbage."

"What's this stuff?"

"It's meat. Just eat what you like."

Kelly looked at the bowl, then methodically went through it, carefully choosing which items to put on her spoon. By the time it made its way to her mouth, Mrs. B already had the answers to three of the down clues and two of the across.

When they had finished their dinner and their game, Kelly put the dominoes back in the box while Mrs. B put the dishes in the sink. Mrs. B took the newspaper to the living room and sat in her rocker to read it. Kelly followed. Mrs. B opened the last section to the comics page and handed it to Kelly.

"Why can't we watch TV?" Kelly asked as she took the paper.

Mrs. B thought about it. It wasn't good to let a child have her way all the time. "Because I like it quiet sometimes."

Kelly looked at the television, then turned and spread the newspaper out on the floor, lying on her stomach so she could see the first comic at the very top. Mrs. B read the local news. Nothing more about Ron Monahan, but of course there wouldn't be. Not until the trial was due, most likely. Eventually, Mrs. B got up and took a pair of scissors from the junk drawer in the kitchen, then came back and started cutting coupons.

Kelly was peering at one of the comics. She looked up. "What's pre C-A-U-T-I-O-N-S mean?"

"Precautions. That's when you plan so something bad doesn't happen."

"Oh." She went back to the comic. Mrs. B cut out a coupon for coffee. It wasn't the brand she liked, but Jimmy next door liked it. She started a second stack.

Kelly looked up again. "This one isn't funny."

Mrs. B put the scissors in her lap and leaned toward Kelly. "What isn't funny?"

"This one." She pointed to a comic.

Mrs. B picked up her scissors again. "They're not all supposed to be funny. Some of them are supposed to make you think."

Kelly frowned. "Well, I think this one's not funny."

When the phone rang, Kelly ran to answer it. "Hi, Mom. Yeah, okay." She hung up and ran to put on her coat. "My mom's home. Bye, Mrs. B."

Mrs. B opened the door for Kelly and stood in the doorway until the girl was safely inside. Then she took her coupons and set them on top of two little stacks next to her microwave. She put the newspaper in the recycling bin, did the dishes, put on her pajamas, turned down the thermostat, settled into bed and picked up the book on her nightstand.

9

It was a Thursday, and it was cold in the kitchen at the Senior Center. While she put the last of the cups in the dishwasher and started on the plates, Mrs. B was making plans to reward herself with a cup of hot cocoa when she and Myrtle finished. It was their turn to clean up after lunch.

Myrtle had her back to Mrs. B, giving the cake platter a quick once-over. She got the last of the crumbs and set the platter on the counter, then grabbed a plate and handed it to Mrs. B.

"I talked to Father," Myrtle whispered, leaning across the dishwasher door.

Mrs. B didn't hear her at first, for the clanging of the plates. When they finished, Myrtle added the soap and turned the machine on. Its usual loud churning began and Mrs. B said, "Did you say something?"

Myrtle nodded. "I talked to Father Clancy. I told him my Ronnie didn't do it. I asked Father, 'Tell me what happened so I can figure out where the money is.' I really meant you, Ed, that you would figure it out, but I told him me. Is that a sin? I lied to a priest. I have to remember to tell that next time I go to confession. I hope I remember.

"Anyhow, Father told me. It was his fault, really, because he got in a fight with her but honestly, she always is so ornery, no matter how nice a day it is outside."

Mrs. B dried her hands on a dishtowel and hung it on the refrigerator door. "What was Father Clancy's fault?"

"He got in a fight with the teller at the bank. That's why the money's gone."

Mrs. B didn't have to ask which teller. Tammy Bartlow, the one with the short red hair, was rude every time she waited on Mrs. B. Mrs. B didn't understand why the bank would keep such a mean person working there, but customer service had certainly changed since her day, so she figured it was some new modern way of doing business. Mrs. B didn't like it, but she didn't expect to like everything.

Myrtle reached up to put the platter on a shelf. Mrs. B said, "I don't follow. Tell me this again."

Myrtle took off her apron and started to fold it. "He didn't want to tell me at first. Father, I mean. I think maybe he was embarrassed, Ed, because he didn't say anything for a while. He just stood there. Then he told me. He got so mad at her, that teller, he took out all the money and said he was going to another bank."

"In cash?" Mrs. B found that hard to believe.

"It was a check. 'Make it out to Cash,' he said. 'I don't know what bank I'm going to, but I'll never set foot in this bank again.' He said something like that." Myrtle paused. "It was a cash check. Maybe not a cash check. Does that sound right, a cash check?"

"A cashier's check?"

"Yes!" Myrtle grabbed Mrs. B's arm. "That was it, a cashier's check. Father was so mad he took the check and went straight to his office and he put it in his desk drawer and he slammed it—he didn't tell me he slammed it, but if I was mad that's what I would do. And then somebody came in and he started doing something else and he forgot about it. And then it was gone."

Mrs. B thought for a minute. "Myrtle, that doesn't make any sense. If that's what happened, why would the police arrest Ron?"

"Because Ronnie has the other key to the desk drawer. He keeps it on his key chain. It's a little key and it's cute, really, sort of round, and it's got a pink cord on it, I don't know why. Anyhow, Ronnie has the other key because Father's always afraid he'll lose his, you know how he is, Ed, and Father had to tell the police because they asked him who else had a key, and he had to say Ronnie because Ronnie has the other key. But I bet Father didn't even lock his desk. He just thought he did."

Myrtle put the apron in a drawer, then turned to Mrs. B. Her eyes glistened with tears. "Will you help me find that money? I don't want my Ronnie to go to jail."

Mrs. B knew what it was like to wake up in the middle of the night worrying about your son. She knew how much that hurt. Where was Leo, right now, right this minute? Asking a stranger for money? Arguing with a policeman? Mrs. B had no way to help him, no way of knowing. Was he cold? Was he lonely? Was he safe? You raise your kids and then they're not yours anymore. But you don't stop loving them, and you never, ever stop being a mom.

"I'll help you, of course I will," Mrs. B said. "I don't know what I can do, but I'll think about what you told me, what Father said. Maybe something will come to mind that will help Ronnie."

There was no harm in giving it some thought. Maybe someone else did take the money. It was a possibility.

Myrtle visibly relaxed, and a tear rolled down her face. She wiped her cheek with the back of her hand. "I bet you can figure out where that money is, Edwina. I know my Ronnie didn't take it. I know his lying face."

10

When Mrs. B got home that evening she turned on the television to watch a movie, but all she could think of was Myrtle's tears.

The first time Leo was arrested, he had just started ninth grade. Leo and Ron and a couple of other boys broke a window at the public school. When the police got there, the boys were in the home economics room making scrambled eggs and toast. Albert thought it was a childish prank, but Mrs. B was devastated. No one in her family had ever been arrested before. She couldn't sleep for days.

Maybe there was something Mrs. B could do to help Myrtle.

The police obviously had evidence that led them to believe Ron Monaghan stole the money from St. Mary's Church. They wouldn't have arrested him otherwise. But what if they were wrong?

Father Clancy told Myrtle the money was in a cashier's check in his desk drawer.

Of course, Father might have lied about that in an attempt to make Myrtle feel better. No, wait, that didn't make sense. If his aim was to comfort Myrtle, he would have said something pastoral. If Father thought Ron took the money, he wouldn't lead Myrtle on. That would be cruel.

If Ron didn't take the money, someone else did.

Mrs. B shut off the TV and went into the kitchen. She made a cup of cocoa, then picked up an old spaghetti sauce jar from the counter and shook out a clump of raisins. She sat back down in her rocker, popped the raisins in her mouth, and thought some more.

It seemed plausible Father didn't lock the desk drawer. When you're angry, you're not thinking straight. And look how he was with his car.

Father Clancy was always forgetting to lock his Cadillac. Once he left the trunk open, and Mrs. B mentioned it to the ladies at the Senior Center while they were having lunch. Rose wasn't surprised at all. She did the linens for the church, and more than once she had taken Father's key chain and gone out to the parking lot to lock the car for him. "People steal cars, you know, Father," she would tell him. And he would always tell her he thought he had locked it.

Anybody who walked into Father's office might have taken that check from the desk drawer.

Before Mrs. B could begin to think of who those people might be, she remembered the office had a large window. If the window was unlocked . . .

News traveled fast in their neighborhood. When Leo was in a fight after school, Mrs. B knew about it before he walked in the front door. Anyone in line at the bank while Father argued with the teller would know about that cashier's check.

The door to the bank opened onto the avenue. The bar was on one side of the bank, Tony's store on the other. If the bank door was opened, people on the avenue could have seen or heard Father Clancy arguing with the teller.

More importantly, it was prime gossip. Anyone who witnessed the argument probably told someone else. Who told someone else. And so on.

Mrs. B blew on her cocoa and took a sip. Goodness, that was no help. Now she had narrowed it down to everyone in Burchfield.

11

By the time Mrs. B got to the Senior Center the next morning, Old Mike was already at the card table sipping his tea. She and Mike were partners the day before, so Mrs. B put her coat on the back of the chair next to him. She opened her mouth to ask him about Father Sean, then closed it again and walked over to the counter for coffee.

When she got back, Mike said, "Were you going to ask me something?"

Mrs. B took a deep breath. "It's just . . . I was thinking about Father Sean. I don't know much about him."

"He's a good Irish boy. From Cork."

"Who?" Vic put his coat on the back of the chair on the other side of Mike.

Mike looked up at him. "Father Sean."

Vic sat down. "He's one of them nancy boys."

"What?" Don hung his coat on the back of his chair, then stood behind it.

"One of them nancy boys," Vic said, taking the cards from the center of the table.

"Who is?" Don asked.

Vic looked up at him. "That Father Sean."

Don snorted. "Where do you get that?"

"Look at him. He has an earring, for chrissake."

"You're an idiot, Vic. My son has an earring and he has three kids." Don rolled his eyes. "Indiana Jones has an earring."

"Indiana Jones doesn't have an earring." Vic handed the cards to Mike. Mike cut them and handed them back.

Don and Vic were into it now. "The wife told me he does," Don said. "Saw him on one of them talk shows."

"Well, he's no better."

"So now it's Indiana Jones? Is that it, Vic? You could take Indiana Jones?"

"Indiana Jones is a nancy boy."

"Indiana Jones is tougher than you'll ever be."

"I could have taken him. I could probably take him now and I'm an old man."

"Jesus, Vic. Come out of the dark ages. An earring don't mean nothing." Vic sat the cards in front of him and got up, and the two of them walked over to get coffee.

Mike turned to Mrs. B. "I don't know a lot about Father Sean, myself. When he first got here somebody told me he was one of them know-it-all jackeens. But he's not from Dublin at all, came to find out, he's from Cork. My grandfather came from Cork, God rest his soul."

He took a sip of his tea. "Seems like a good boy, Father Sean. Always raising money to send back to Ireland. For some cause, can't remember the name. Never heard of it before. He hit me up once, but I give my charity money to St. Vincent de Paul. They helped my sainted mother after the St. Patrick's Day Flood."

12

As Mrs. B was on her way to sit with her friends for lunch, Lily called her to the mahjong table and gestured toward a little woman across from her.

"She wants to know where you got your sweatshirt," Lily said.

Mrs. B looked down to see what she was wearing. It was the white sweatshirt with the rooster on it. "My neighbor bought it for me. I think he got it at a flea market." Every time Jimmy went to the flea market, he brought something home for Mrs. B. Usually it was puzzle books. She had no idea why he thought this sweatshirt suited her, but it certainly was warm.

Lily spoke in Chinese to the woman, then turned back to Mrs. B. "She likes roosters." The little woman smiled, and Mrs. B smiled back.

When she finally got to the lunch table her tray was starting to feel heavy, and Mrs. B put it down with a thud.

"I was just talking about you," Myrtle said as Mrs. B pulled out her chair.

Anne looked up from her plate and caught Mrs. B's eye. Rose nodded hello and went back to picking through her green beans, looking for the almonds.

Myrtle went on. "I told them you're going to find out who stole that money from the church. So my Ronnie won't have to go to jail."

Mrs. B pretended to be interested in her chicken and gravy. Oh, my goodness. This was embarrassing. She thought maybe she should respond but, for the life of her, she didn't know what to say. She finally looked up and Anne caught her worried glance.

Anne looked closely at Mrs. B for a few seconds. Then she got a twinkle in her eye and turned to Myrtle. "That's great," Anne said seriously. "No one wants your Ronnie to go to jail." She picked up a roll and started to butter it. "Well. That's settled, then. Ed will take care of it. Do we have cherry pie for dessert? I thought someone said there was cherry pie, but I didn't see any."

Mrs. B turned to Anne, visibly relieved. "Don said the delivery truck is late, but they're bringing cherry pie. It's left over from yesterday at the supermarket."

Rose looked at Mrs. B and smiled, then looked down at her plate. She took a forkful of mashed potatoes. Mrs. B did the same.

"I do like cherry pie," Rose said.

13

On her way home, Myrtle's announcement weighed on Mrs. B's mind. She was grateful to Anne for changing the subject at the lunch table. It crossed her mind, just for a split second, that maybe she should say something to Myrtle. And just as quickly, the thought was gone.

Mrs. B knew she'd never say anything. To someone else, yes, of course she would. She'd tell them how inappropriate it was, how embarrassing it was. But Myrtle—she couldn't say something like that to her. Myrtle didn't mean anything by it. Myrtle was always, always trying to please, always so careful to be considerate, to be generous, to be kind. Even though words flew out of her mouth like popcorn, Mrs. B couldn't remember ever hearing Myrtle say an unkind thing. And look how she'd started crying at just the *thought* of her friends at the Senior Center talking about her. If Mrs. B said anything to Myrtle . . . well, it was a moot point. It would be like stepping on a kitten. Mrs. B would never do that.

She got to the front door and put her key in the lock. Maybe there really was something she could think of to help Ron's lawyer. Anything might be helpful, really. Anything that could point toward reasonable doubt.

Walking through her front door, Mrs. B tossed her coat onto the loveseat and looked through the mail. The gas bill went in her top dresser drawer, next to her checkbook. An envelope from a charity she never heard of went unopened into the recycling bin. She started to open a letter from her daughter Helen, then changed her mind and put it on her bed stand. Helen always wrote such nice letters. She'd save it to read right before she went to bed.

In the kitchen, she poured some coffee left over from the morning and put it in the microwave. When it was warm, she added milk, took the cup to the living room and curled up in the barcalounger to think. She mentally went over her list of suspects from the night before, then remembered she had made the list longer instead of shorter.

She had to take a new tack. She took a sip of coffee and as it warmed her throat she thought, Okay . . . on a normal day, who has access to Father's desk?

Ron wouldn't have any reason to be in the parish office unless there was a board meeting or construction being done. He wouldn't make the list.

Rose is there once a week to pick up the linens and bring back the clean ones. She could have gone in. Rose had regular access to the parish office and the rectory. No one would ever question her being there.

Rose was so mysterious, too. Never talked about herself at all. It certainly was odd that no one knew where she grew up or anything about her life before she got married. Maybe Rose had a secret problem. Or shady characters in her past.

Immediately, Mrs. B felt a pang of guilt. Why on earth would Rose steal money from the church? For goodness sake, she's from a family of policemen! Mrs. B had lunch with Rose every day. Rose was a perfectly nice lady. She just liked to keep her business to herself. Which maybe more people should. Mrs. B was ashamed of herself for suspecting her friend.

It would have been easier on her conscience to suspect Vic. Vic was just plain ornery. But Mrs. B couldn't think of a reason Vic would be in the parish office.

Father Sean was in the parish office every day. It certainly was convenient he was called away right when the money disappeared. Would Father Clancy cover up for the young priest? No, Mrs. B didn't think he would. Especially not if it meant Ron Monaghan would go to jail for a crime he didn't commit. Father and Ron had been close since Ron was a boy. Mrs. B knew there was a genuine affection between them. If he knew anything that would exonerate Ron, she was sure Father Clancy would have told the police.

Mrs. B finished her coffee and set the cup on the end table, then reached over to the corner of her couch for an afghan. She pulled the lever on the chair and leaned back as it reclined.

Before she started thinking all her friends were thieves, it might make sense to see if she could find something out about Father Sean. Maybe look on the internet.

Mrs. B pictured herself at one of the computers at the Senior Center, then realized anyone who walked by would be able to see what she was doing.

Tomorrow was Saturday. She could go to the library downtown. They had computers there.

She settled back in the barcalounger, pulled the afghan to her chin, and took a nap.

14

When Mrs. B awoke it was almost six. She checked the phone to see if there were messages. There weren't any. *Dobrze,* she thought in the Polish language of her youth. Good.

She looked over the frozen dinners in her freezer. After some deliberation she decided on the turkey tetrazzini. Prying off the corner of the cellophane covering the plastic tray, she put the tray on a plate and popped it into the microwave.

She started a fresh pot of coffee. She took a mug from the china hutch, poured some milk into it, and put it on the kitchen table. Then she sat down to work on what was left of the morning's crossword puzzle.

When the little ding came eight minutes later, she opened the microwave and pulled out the plate with a worn yellow potholder mitt, careful not to let her fingers come through the hole. She placed it on a tray and added her cup of coffee, a package of fruit cocktail from the refrigerator, a napkin, a fork and her favorite spoon. She headed back to the living room.

When she turned on the television, there was a Cary Grant picture already in progress. She remembered the plot from the last time she saw it, and settled into her rocking chair with the TV tray in front of her. She took a bite of the turkey tetrazzini. *Dobrze.* She had a good life.

15

The next morning, Mrs. B ate cereal in front of the TV news, waiting for the weather report. The afghan that had been on her lap was now on the love seat. After raising the thermostat a half hour ago, the house was finally starting to warm up.

There was a silly story about a monkey, and then the weatherman finally appeared. Snow today, accumulation one to two inches. Tomorrow sunny. She shut off the TV and took another bite of the cereal. She didn't think the snow would stick. It was too early in the season. Still, she'd be foolish to risk it.

So, no trip downtown today. She'd have to go next week. As a schoolgirl she had been adventurous, even daring, in the snow. Her childhood neighborhood was full of steep hills, and traversing them every day made her bold, even on ice.

But that was then. Now she was an old lady who had to worry about slipping and falling and breaking a hip. Well, that was fair. She'd had her day.

She went into the kitchen, poured another cup of coffee, and picked up a book from her bookshelf.

At four o'clock she turned on the news again, and they led with the weather. The meteorologist recanted his earlier prediction, which didn't surprise her at all since there hadn't been a snowflake all day. "Snow after midnight," he said, pointing at the green and red clouds traveling along his map. "Two to four inches."

Four inches could be enough to stick. Mrs. B got up to get her coat. She'd better go to four-thirty Mass tonight. She could be snowed in tomorrow.

<u>16</u>

At the end of Mass, Father surprised the congregation by walking to the pulpit and addressing them again.

"The ushers will be handing out the *City Catholic* newspaper this week. I know we usually have them in stacks in the vestibule, but we want to make sure you all get one. There is a story of importance on the front page. I don't want anyone to be alarmed. The board has known about this for weeks, and we have been working closely with the diocese to do everything we can to make sure our interests are protected.

"The Mass is ended. Go in peace."

"Thanks be to God," Mrs. B responded with the congregation as she buttoned her coat. She pulled her babushka out of her pocket and put it on her head as the recessional hymn began, and slowly made her way up the aisle.

"Here you go, Mrs. B," said one of the ushers as he handed her the diocesan newspaper. She tucked it under her arm and braced herself for the cold evening air.

17

Back home, Mrs. B sat in her rocker and unfolded the City Catholic. The headline read, "Church Closings Imminent."

Mrs. B's eyes scanned down to the bottom of the page to a section titled Under Consideration. Churches were listed in alphabetical order. St. Mary's was eighth on the list.

She went back to the beginning and read the article carefully.

The bishop was reviewing the effectiveness of twelve churches. The list was crafted carefully last spring at the annual meeting of the secretariats. At the time of its creation this list was simply a contingency measure, but the economic situation of the diocese now dictated serious deliberation of the issue.

Considerations would include the size of the parish, its fiscal health, and its proximity to other active churches.

Parishioners must remember the economy is not what it used to be. Congregations are much smaller than they were when these churches were built. These discussions may be unpleasant, but parishioners should realize they were inevitable. When a decision is made, five of the churches under discussion must close.

Mrs. B put the paper in the recycling bin.

Though she told herself that five in twelve gave them better than even odds, Mrs. B tossed and turned and woke up twice that night.

18

It did snow early Sunday morning, but not much. By afternoon it had melted away.

At cards on Monday, Old Mike sat quietly drinking his tea. Mrs. B shifted uncomfortably in her chair while the two of them watched Don and Vic.

Vic shook his head vehemently. "Well, if they close the church they'll close the Senior Center."

"No, they won't. The city will find a place for us."

"Bullshit. The city just laid off those park employees. They don't have a pot to piss in."

"They can't leave us without a senior center." Don was getting hot under the collar.

Vic was adamant. "Mount Oak doesn't have a senior center. Hightop doesn't have a senior center."

Don didn't want to hear it. "Well, St. Mary's isn't going to close anyhow. We have plenty of people coming to our church. Saint hickymajigger, the one with the arrows . . . "

Mike moved the string on his teabag to the other side of his cup. "Sebastian."

"Saint Sebastian. They hardly have anybody in their parish any more. My cousin Josie said there were fifteen people at church there last Sunday."

"So what. They're closing five. They still need four more. We are on the list." He said the last sentence slowly, emphasizing each word, then leaned back in his chair. Don put the cards in front of him. Vic cut them and put them in front of Don.

After a moment, Vic looked up. "Know what, Don? This *one* time, you might know what you're talking about. I bet we're on that list 'cause the bishop and those diocesan guys wanted to get their grubby hands on all that money old Doc Harrigan gave us. And now it's gone." Vic slammed his palm down on the table. "Serves them right."

After cards, when Don and Vic headed toward lunch, Mike turned to Mrs. B. "Yesterday, one of the ushers at church told me Myrtle told him you're going to keep her son out of jail. That you're going to find out who really took the money from the church."

Mrs. B looked at Mike in surprise. Again, she didn't know what to say.

Luckily, Mike didn't seem to be looking for a response. "No one wants to believe their grown child would do something bad. But sometimes they do." He shook his head sadly. "Sometimes they do."

19

The article in the *City Catholic* was a topic of conversation among the ladies, too. If they were scared, though, they didn't show it.

"We have a nice church. St. Mary's might not be the prettiest church on the list, but we have Father Clancy." Anne punctuated her words with her fork as she talked.

Rose replied, "That's true. Father Clancy has been here a long, long time. Some of those other churches get a new pastor every couple of years, seems like."

"And we have a lot of people come to our church," Anne said. "It's not full on Sundays like it used to be, but on Christmas it's full. For late Mass, anyhow. And on Easter it's full."

Mrs. B said, "Everybody comes to see their mother on Easter."

Myrtle chimed in. "And then everybody comes to St. Mary's. It's nice when it's full. I like that song they sing at Easter, what is it?"

"'Jesus Christ Is Risen Today'?" Anne asked.

"Yes, that's so pretty." Myrtle bobbed her head back and forth as she sang, "Jesus Christ is risen todaaaaay, Aaaaaa-le-luuu-ia."

Mrs. B smiled. "That is a pretty song."

Rose said, "I like that one."

Myrtle said, "I think that's my very favorite Easter song. They always play the organ too slow but it still sounds pretty. I like all the alleluias."

"Me, too," Anne said.

"Me, too," said Rose.

Anne said, "I think they might close Saint Barnabas. Hardly anybody lives in Polk anymore. There's all kinds of empty houses. Remember when we used to get our school uniforms there?"

"I remember that," Mrs. B said. "Every summer your mom would take you over and they would measure you. Then you would get your uniform before school started and it would be too big so you could grow into it." She turned to Rose and ventured, "Did you get your school uniform in Polk?"

Rose replied, "Maybe. I don't remember."

Mrs. B thought about asking Rose where she went to school but before she made up her mind, Anne came back to the subject at hand. "I wish they didn't have to close any churches."

"Me, too," said Myrtle.

"Me, too," Mrs. B and Rose said in unison.

20

As they left the Senior Center, Mrs. B pulled the knot in her babushka a little tighter and put on her gloves while Myrtle told her about the turkey she was planning to get for Thanksgiving.

"It's just me and Ronnie, and the grandkids will come over later, but they'll only eat ice cream or peach pie. I know everybody makes pumpkin pie but my kids always liked peach pie so I make peach pie and now we always have peach pie. And we'll have ice cream.

"My Annie and my Michael aren't coming but they're coming for Christmas so it'll just be me and

Ronnie. So I'm getting a turkey breast, not a whole turkey. I'm going to cook it in the crockpot with cranberry sauce. I never did that before but I saw it in a magazine and I'm going to try it. Since it's just me and Ronnie." Mrs. B could see Myrtle's breath as she talked. "Is your Helen coming?"

"No, I don't think so," Mrs. B said. "I just had a letter from her. If she was coming for Thanksgiving she would have mentioned it."

"Do you want to eat with us?" Myrtle asked.

Mrs. B wondered if she should lie. The truth was the classic movie channel was scheduled to show Bing Crosby movies all day on Thanksgiving. Mrs. B had been looking forward to it all month.

She turned to her friend. "Thank you, Myrtle, but I'd rather stay home. I like to have a day to myself every once in a while, and I'm looking forward to relaxing and watching television that day."

They waited at the stop sign. "Well, okay, Edwina. I don't always understand you, but if that's what you want to do."

As they made their way across the avenue, Myrtle said, "I don't want you to be lonely. If you get lonely on Thanksgiving, you can call me and come up for supper. If it's snowing, Ronnie can come down with his car so you don't have to walk."

"I promise you, if I feel lonely that day, I will call you," Mrs. B said.

"You might change your mind," Myrtle said. "Let me know if you change your mind and you can come over." Mrs. B nodded as she turned toward home.

21

Mrs. B settled into her rocker and picked up a news magazine from her coffee table. Her daughter had given her a subscription for Christmas, after Mrs. B told her she admired the unbiased way this particular magazine reported the news. It was beyond the means of her own pocketbook, and Mrs. B had appreciated Helen's little extravagance.

Until today.

Halfway through an article about a young politician, Mrs. B started to get angry. These journalists ought to know better. It was their job to know better. Mrs. B finished the article but, in her opinion, most of it belonged on the editorial page.

As she wondered if the magazine's new owner was responsible for this irritating breach, her phone rang. She went to the hallway and picked up the receiver.

"Hello."

No answer. Must be one of those phone solicitors. They never answer right away. "Hello?"

The voice was muffled and she couldn't hear what was being said. "Could you speak up? I can't understand you."

The voice was louder but still muffled. She could just make it out. "Heave it a bone," it sounded like.

"I don't have a dog," she said. She hung up. What a stupid way to advertise dog food. She didn't understand business at all anymore.

The phone rang again. She let it ring a few times. At the third ring, she picked up the receiver.

"Hello?" Mrs. B wondered if she sounded testy, then decided she didn't care if she did.

"Mom?"

To her surprise, it was her daughter's voice. "Oh, Helen. Hi, honey."

"What's the matter, Mom? You don't sound right."

"Oh, I'm fine. I just hung up on a phone solicitor."

"You shouldn't be getting those calls anymore. I put you on a do-not-call list."

"Tell them that." Mrs. B caught herself. "I'm sorry, honey. I don't mean to take it out on you. I just didn't like the person's tone of voice."

Helen was quiet for a few seconds. "Mom, are you sure everything is alright?"

"Absolutely. Everything is fine. Why did you call? I just got your letter a couple of days ago. Did something happen?"

"No, no, nothing like that. I called to ask you a favor."

Mrs. B waited.

"Mom? Are you still there?"

"I'm waiting to see what the favor is."

"Oh. Well, Malcolm's mother is having her 85th birthday, and you know she was born around Christmas time."

Mrs. B's heart sank.

"So we were wondering if we could come visit at Easter instead of Christmas this year."

Mrs. B paused. That wasn't too bad. It wasn't like she'd decided not to come at all. "That's fine, honey."

"Are you disappointed?"

"Of course I am. But it's fine. Easter isn't that far off. And you have a responsibility to your husband

and his family." Even if you live near them and they get to see you all the time, she thought.

"Thanks, Mom. I knew you'd understand. I'll tell Malcolm." There was a noise in the background while her daughter spoke. It sounded like a buzzer. Helen asked again, "Everything is really alright there?"

"Yes, everything is fine. I'm unhappy with that news magazine you gave me, but that's about it."

"I thought you liked that magazine. What's the matter with it?"

"Oh, I'll tell you in a letter. It will give me something to write about."

"Mom, I have to go. There's someone at the door. Thanks for being so understanding. I'll . . . " The buzzer sounded again, repeatedly. "I've got to go. I'll write soon. Bye."

Mrs. B put down the receiver and stood and looked at the phone for a minute. Then she went back to her rocker and picked up the magazine.

She hadn't been reading for five minutes when someone knocked at the door. "What is this, Grand Central Station?" she said aloud as she got up again.

Kelly was standing on her doorstep with a backpack. "Can I do my homework here? Julie and Patrick are kissing on the couch. They think I can't see them from the kitchen table but I can."

Mrs. B opened the door and stepped aside. "Come on in. Julie knows you're over here, right?" she said as she made her way back to her chair and turned on the television.

Kelly nodded as she pulled a lined sheet of paper out of her backpack. It had a gold star stuck to it, and an A at the top in red ink. "I got an A on my arithmetic. Look."

Mrs. B took the paper from her and read it through. "This one was pretty hard." She pointed to a problem. "Good job, Kelly. You should be proud of yourself."

Kelly took the paper back and looked at it. Mrs. B said, "It feels good when you get an A, doesn't it?"

"Yeah," Kelly said, picking at the edges of the gold star. She turned to look at the television. "What are you watching?"

"A movie." Mrs. B picked up her magazine from the coffee table.

"Why does it look like that?" Kelly asked.

"Like what?"

"You know, everybody's gray."

Mrs. B turned to the page she had dog-eared when she answered the door. "It's in black and white. That's how movies used to look. They couldn't always make them in color. It was expensive then."

Kelly stared at the TV for a minute. "Can we watch something else?"

"No."

"Why not?"

Mrs. B was dividing her attention between the television and the magazine in her lap. "Because it's my house. If we were at your house, you could be in charge." She was trying to decide whether to warm up her coffee or just drink it cold. "Don't you have homework to do?"

"Yeah." Kelly looked at her backpack and then at the coffee table. "Can I have something to drink?"

"Help yourself. You know where everything is." Kelly went into the kitchen. By the time Mrs. B decided to put her coffee in the microwave, the little girl was carefully pouring a glass of orange juice.

When Mrs. B got back to the living room, Kelly was kneeling on the floor. Her backpack was on the love seat. Schoolbooks and papers covered the coffee table. Kelly had a pencil in one hand and was leaning over a workbook.

Mrs. B sat down with her coffee and said, "Let me know if I can help you with anything."

Kelly looked up. "This one's easy."

Mrs. B went back to her magazine.

By seven thirty, Kelly had packed up her books, and she and Mrs. B were watching a sitcom rerun.

At the loud grumble of a motorcycle engine outside, Kelly ran to the window and looked out.

"My mom's home. Bye, Mrs. B," she said over her shoulder as she flung open the door.

Mrs. B pointed. "Don't forget your bookbag."

The little girl grabbed her backpack and coat, and ran out the door.

I'll bet Kelly will never leave *her* mom, Mrs. B thought as she watched her cross the street. I'll bet when Michele is old and gray, Kelly will live right next door.

22

The wind whipped through Mrs. B's coat while she stood at the bus stop. She leaned on the mailbox and set her cane next to it. Most of the time the cane was a nuisance, but she had gotten into the habit of taking it on longer trips in case she needed it for balance.

When the bus finally arrived, ten minutes later, Mrs. B pulled herself aboard with both hands and sat in a seat near the driver. Leaning the cane beside her, she unbuttoned the top two buttons of her coat, put her good purse in her lap and took off her gloves.

She looked around. Not many people on the bus.

Saturdays used to be shopping days, movie days. Now everyone went to the mall.

Years ago, when she was a career gal, Mrs. B rode the bus every day. Now she only rode on rare occasions. Usually to shop. This was the first time she'd ridden the bus to do surreptitious research on a young priest at the downtown branch of the library.

She settled into her seat and turned to her right to look out the window, and the simple gesture brought back memories.

Mrs. B used to love working in an office—the smell of the mimeograph machine, the pneumatic tubes that took your mail from floor to floor, the phones ringing, the hustle and bustle. It made her feel like she was part of something important.

Walking through the big glass doors on her first day at Lava Crucible, Mrs. B was a little leery. Her new boss was a woman, and all the girls from secretarial college warned her that a lady boss was the absolute worst. But it turned out that wasn't true at all. She and Miss Harvey got along famously.

Mrs. B's business school training helped her to learn the new bookkeeping machines right away, and her shorthand came in handy when she was making confidential notes about the payroll while the men from the executive level were walking by.

Before long she was Miss Harvey's right-hand gal. Miss Harvey was the first person to call her Ed. Mrs. B liked the clipped, efficient sound of it. The name stuck.

When the bus went through the railroad trestle and turned right, Mrs. B's thoughts took her back to the day Albert came downtown, on leave from the service, to take her to lunch. He looked so smart in his uniform. Miss Harvey gave her an extra hour off—it was her patriotic duty, she said with a smile.

Miss Harvey winked at Albert as the couple left, arm in arm. They went to the cafeteria in Market Square and had a grand time that afternoon, laughing and talking. They ate three pieces of cherry pie between them.

As he walked her back to work, Albert steered them toward the Clark Building, where they oohed and aahed over the jewelry in the window. He was planning all along to ask me to marry him, she remembered thinking later. He popped the question the next evening, with a ring she had admired. She said yes.

She looked out the window at the river, where the steel mill used to be. They were almost downtown. She put her gloves back on, buttoned her coat and pulled the yellow cord as the driver approached her stop.

23

The library was two blocks down, past the department store and the bank. Tall buildings blocked her from the wind so Mrs. B took her time walking, taking in the Christmas displays in the shop windows.

At two minutes before ten, she reached the door of the library and joined the queue waiting for the doors to open. A young woman in a yellow sweater let them in precisely at ten o'clock. Hanging the string of keys around her neck, she held the door and stepped aside for the little throng.

Mrs. B walked in and looked around. She hadn't been to the downtown branch of the library since they remodeled, and it was a little disconcerting.

The books were in stacks to her left and there was lots of open space in the center, with bright lights and white laminate tables everywhere. People were talking right out loud, not in whispers. The whole effect was more like a coffee shop than a library.

She walked to a long, shiny white counter that spanned half the room, stopping in front of a busy-looking woman in her fifties with bright red hair. The librarian looked at her computer screen for a few seconds before she turned to Mrs. B.

"Yes, can I help you?" the woman said in a formal way that suggested it was the last thing in the world she wanted to do.

"I'd like to use a computer, please."

"That way." She pointed toward the young woman in the yellow sweater, who appeared to be switching on six computers near a staircase.

Mrs. B walked back and sat at the first computer at the end of the row. She leaned her cane against the table and put her purse on the floor beside her.

The young woman in the yellow sweater came running over. "Would you like some help?" she asked sweetly. "Or are you okay on your own?"

I must look like I need help, Mrs. B thought. It must show. She said, "I want to look for something."

"It will help if you tell me what you'd like to find," the librarian said cheerfully.

Mrs. B wondered why she was being hesitant. The young woman couldn't care less what Mrs. B was looking for. She was simply trying to do her job.

"I'm looking for information about a person."

"We'll log you in first. Do you have your library card?"

Mrs. B reached down for her purse and pulled out the card. The librarian showed her where to type the library card number into the computer.

The young woman said, "Okay, then. Let's type your person's name into a search engine." She reached for the computer mouse over Mrs. B's shoulder and clicked on a little logo. A page appeared with a blank in the center.

"Okay, type in the name and we'll see what comes up."

Mrs. B typed Sean Flaherty. A list of blue underlined paragraphs came onto the screen. Most were about a musician. Two were about a politician from Massachusetts.

The young woman leaned over Mrs. B's shoulder. "Did you find the person you're looking for?"

"No. Goodness, can you find someone if they have a common name?"

"Sure, if you add qualifiers. Do you know where he lives, or anything else distinctive we might use to narrow it down?"

"He's a priest."

"That should help."

"And he's from Ireland."

"Well, type 'Father Sean Flaherty Ireland' and we'll see what we get."

Mrs. B hit the enter button, and a new page full of blue paragraphs appeared. She looked them over as the librarian went to the checkout counter to answer the phone.

The first blue paragraph led to an article on a BBC website. A splinter group of the IRA had claimed responsibility for a bombing at the Tin and Penny Pub in Ulster after the World Cup. The group's known members were listed, including a Father Sean Flaherty.

Oh, my goodness.

She read further. Fortunately, the bomb was not built properly. It only broke a few bottles. No one was injured.

If this was their Father Sean, he certainly wasn't very good at being a criminal.

She read through a few more articles, most of them about the same IRA splinter group and this particular bombing attempt. Mrs. B read them slowly and carefully, but couldn't find any sure evidence that this was her Father Sean. Nor any evidence it wasn't.

A little timer appeared to say she had five more minutes on the computer. She clicked on the last blue paragraph.

The article was from the British newspaper *The Guardian*. It had more details on this splinter group, who called themselves Ireland's Liberators. They had been linked to bombings since the peace talks began. Though their last few bombing attempts were unsuccessful, all members of the organization were considered highly dangerous.

Britain's MI5 was in pursuit, and three members of Ireland's Liberators had been arrested in the past year. It was believed to be a small group, less than fifty members. The terrorist organization was distinguished by the fact that they refused to traffic drugs to fund their activities as did other splinter groups. Instead, they were funded by aid they received from supporters in the United States.

Mrs. B read the line again.

There is conclusive evidence that Ireland's Liberators are funded by aid they receive from supporters in the United States.

Oh, my. Mrs. B's heart began to beat faster. She stopped to take a deep breath just as the article disappeared and the log-in page appeared.

Mrs. B stared at the now-blank screen. A few minutes passed. Finally, she reached down and picked up her purse and cane. She walked by the counter and said thank you to the young woman in the yellow sweater, who nodded as she talked to someone on the phone. Then she buttoned her coat and went out into the cold again.

24

She didn't know anything yet. Not really.

Mrs. B walked to the corner and waited for the light. She opened her purse to make sure she had the gift card Helen sent for her birthday. It was there, in the little pocket with her keys. She closed her purse again.

A small group began to congregate at the corner. A mom held the hand of a little boy while her other hand pushed a baby in a stroller. A businessman stood importantly with his briefcase.

They all moved together when the light changed. The businessman walked briskly toward the office building ahead of them. The woman with the stroller walked toward the bus stop. Mrs. B smiled at the baby as they passed. Then she opened the door of the bookstore.

Well, she did know a few things. A priest named Sean Flaherty is a member of a terrorist group called Ireland's Liberators. They get their money from the United States.

Money is missing from the church.

Father Sean is back in Ireland.

The bookstore was large, larger than the library. It was her first time there, and when Mrs. B walked in she didn't know where to turn. To her left was what looked like a little cafe. Two people sat at the same table, typing on portable computers and ignoring each other. To her right was a counter with a line roped off, the type of line Mrs. B was used to seeing at a theater or a bank. There was no one waiting, and the two clerks were talking on their cell phones.

She saw an information sign in the center of the store and walked toward it. Beneath the sign was a young man with a round face, dark-rimmed glasses and a haircut that stood up. He looked like an owl. He smiled as she approached the yellow counter.

"Can you tell me where I'd find children's books?" she asked.

"They're to your left in the back of the store. Are you looking for anything in particular?" He turned toward a computer, hands poised over the keys.

"No, I'd just like to browse. And where are biographies?"

The young man pointed toward the left, but not as far back. She had a sudden urge to think of a question that would make him say, "Whooo?" She knew she would never do it but the temptation made her grin. She thanked him and headed toward the back of the store.

Mrs. B had come to the bookstore on a mission. The last time Kelly was at her house, Mrs. B learned that her little neighbor didn't know what an encyclopedia was. She was determined to remedy that.

She thought she'd browse the children's books awhile to see if she could find something suitable. The books were categorized so neatly, and the selection so large, that it didn't take long. In a few minutes she was cradling the *Scholastic Children's Encyclopedia* in the crook of her arm and heading toward the biography section, her thoughts again on Ireland's Liberators.

Father Sean left just when the money disappeared from the church. But that was all Mrs. B knew for sure. Maybe it meant something. Maybe it didn't.

It took Mrs. B the better part of an hour to choose a book for herself. She picked up a biography of Bette Davis, but it looked a little tawdry. A biography of Pope John Paul II looked a little dry. How can you write a boring book about such an exciting life, she wondered as she placed it back on the shelf.

Finally, she made her way to the romances and was surprised to find a book by Mary Stewart she hadn't yet read.

After that, she chose a book to send to Helen for Christmas, a large one about decorating. She felt a wave of sadness as she carried it with her other books to the cashier's line at the front of the store. Mrs. B didn't relish the idea of spending Christmas alone. Even worse would be to play the part of "the poor old lady with no one to spend Christmas with" at someone else's dinner table.

She looked down at the children's encyclopedia and stopped in her tracks. Why not invite Kelly and Michele over for Christmas?

The idea cheered her up. She mentally added the price of the books she was carrying and subtracted it from the amount of the gift card. Then she went over to a display in the cafe and grabbed a tin of fancy tea for Michele.

As she walked to the cashier's counter, it gave her a certain satisfaction to spend Helen's money on gifts for her new neighbors. She felt a little guilty, but it also felt a little good. It only seemed fair.

"Shopping, Ed?" Jimmy asked as he got out of his car. Mrs. B had made it up the street just as the first few snowflakes were falling.

"I went downtown and picked up some Christmas presents."

"I never go downtown anymore," Jimmy said. "I always go to the mall." He locked the car and put the keys in his pocket, then turned toward her. "I'll take you grocery shopping later in the week. Want to switch coupons now? That'll give us a couple days to look through them all. We won't have to rush like last time."

"Absolutely," Mrs. B said and went into her house to get the stack of coupons by the microwave.

25

Mrs. B's cart was wobbly. She thumbed through the coupons in her purse until she found the one for tomato sauce. Checking the expiration date on the coupon, she switched the can in her cart for another on the shelf.

Jimmy was still in the produce aisle, picking out a cantaloupe. Mrs. B would never buy a cantaloupe in the wintertime. It didn't seem right somehow. Winter was for apples and oranges and canned pumpkin.

Canned pumpkin. She looked at it for a little bit, then walked on by. Canned corn, green beans, beets went into her cart. Ketchup. Macaroni. She made her way to the meat counter and got a family-sized package of ground beef. She could make *klops* for tonight and cook the rest and freeze it, then add it to spaghetti sauce or cabbage soup.

When her children were young, on their birthdays Mrs. B made their favorite dinner. Leo always wanted *klops* and mashed potatoes. Helen liked chicken pot pie.

When Helen came home from college freshman year, she started calling *klops* "Salisbury steak." Mrs. B didn't like it. It made her feel sad, like Helen was ashamed to be Polish.

At the poultry case, Mrs. B found a nice chicken breast for Thanksgiving. Past the turkeys there was a display of hams. She picked up a small one. Perfect. She backtracked to the canned foods for pineapple rings and maraschino cherries.

Well, I'm certainly getting my exercise. I'm all over the place, she thought as she walked through the beverage aisle. A bottle of ginger ale went into her cart.

She looked at her list. Paper towels and t.p., and she'd be all done. After the paper aisle, she went looking for Jimmy. He was a few aisles behind her, a box of cereal in each hand.

It would be a little while before he was ready to go home. Just enough time, she decided, for a little reward. She headed toward the bakery for a big, iced cinnamon bun.

At the checkout she spotted Jimmy in line two aisles down, talking with Rose. Mrs. B stared at them for a moment, then realized she was staring and turned away. Curious. Jimmy quit going to church years ago. How would he know Rose?

Rose looked over and caught Mrs. B's eye. She smiled and waved, and Mrs. B waved back. Jimmy turned around, then went back to their conversation.

When Mrs. B and Jimmy were settled into the car and Mrs. B was finished struggling with her seat belt, she asked, "How do you know Rose?"

"Who?" Jimmy asked.

"Rose."

"Who's Rose?"

"The lady you were just talking to."

Jimmy pulled out of the parking lot. "When?"

"In line just now."

"Oh. I don't know her. I don't think I do. She did look familiar, like maybe I knew her from when we were younger. Did she go to St. Mary's?"

"No, I don't think so," Mrs. B said. "I'm pretty sure she moved to Burchfield when she got married."

"Oh. I could have met her when we were teenagers. Maybe saw her at a dance or something."

Mrs. B went into her purse and got out a butterscotch. She asked Jimmy if he wanted one. When he nodded she unwrapped two, handed one to him and popped the other in her mouth.

Jimmy said, "We were looking at a magazine cover. Me and that lady, Rose. Then we started talking about *General Hospital*."

After that, Mrs. B and Jimmy began to itemize the ways in which *General Hospital* was not as good as *Guiding Light* used to be. The discussion lasted until they passed St. Mary's, where four men were assembling a wooden platform on the sidewalk outside the church.

"Must be for the parade," Jimmy said.

"Oh, that's right, it's tomorrow night," Mrs. B said. "They were talking about it at the Senior Center. Danny McCoy's coming in. His mom's birthday's this weekend, I think."

"He's a big deal, that Danny, now that he's coaching the Bears." Jimmy pulled in to the empty parking spot in front of his house. As they were getting their bags from the trunk, Michele was walking from her front door to her car. Mrs. B put down the bag with the orange juice and crossed the street.

"Hi, Michele."

"Oh, hi, Mrs. B." The young woman seemed to be in a hurry.

Mrs. B said, "I thought you might like to know there's a Christmas parade tomorrow night down the avenue. My kids used to love it."

Michele turned toward her while opening the car door. "Thanks. I have to work but maybe I can get Julie to take Kelly."

Mrs. B thought for a second about Kelly and Julie. Then she said, "If Kelly wants to go, tell her to stop by my house. I can take her down."

Michele was already getting into her car. "Okay, thanks, Mrs. B," she said.

Unpacking her groceries in the kitchen, Mrs. B wondered why she had said that. It was going to be cold out tomorrow night, and she hadn't been to the parade in years. Oh well, too late now.

In the last bag was the cinnamon bun. She rinsed the coffeepot in the sink and started a fresh pot. I wonder what's on TV, she thought, as she waited for it to brew.

26

Before it was dark on Saturday, Kelly was already at Mrs. B's door.

"Hi, Mrs. B!" The little girl was practically jumping up and down, and Mrs. B couldn't help but laugh.

"Hi, honey. Come on in."

Kelly stood stock still. "Julie said you were taking me to the parade."

"It doesn't start for a while yet." Mrs. B took her by the shoulder and brought her into the living room. "Come in and shut the door. You're letting all the cold air in."

Kelly sat on the couch with her coat on. "But we have to leave soon, right? It starts soon, right?"

"We'll leave pretty soon." Mrs. B picked up her newspaper and handed Kelly the comics. Kelly glanced at the newspaper, then put it on the coffee table. She took her shoes off and sat back on the couch.

"Take off your coat, you'll get overheated. We can't go yet. It's too early."

Kelly looked at her.

Mrs. B said, "We'll leave soon, I promise. Just not yet."

Kelly shrugged off her coat and went to the bookshelf. She picked up the box of dominoes and, crawling back up on the couch, sat cross-legged in one corner, pulling out tiles and arranging them in patterns on the couch cushion. She had a pretty intricate web going when Mrs. B stood up and got her coat and hat.

"Do you have to go to the bathroom before we leave?" Mrs. B asked.

"No, I don't have to go," Kelly said.

"Are you sure?"

"Positive," Kelly said as she hurriedly pulled on her shoes. Mrs. B helped her with the zipper on her coat, pulled the hood up and stepped back to look at her. Then she grabbed a green knit scarf from her coat rack and wrapped it around Kelly's neck. Kelly shook her head around as Mrs. B tied it.

Mrs. B reached into her purse to get her key and handkerchief and put them in her coat pocket. "Okay, let's go."

The two of them walked to the bottom of the street, Kelly dancing two steps to every one of Mrs. B's, first running ahead, then backtracking, then running ahead again. Mrs. B walked at her usual pace, happy that the evening wasn't too cold and the sidewalks were clear.

They passed a few teenagers and a young couple with a baby stroller. Mrs. B didn't know them. Must have parked here for the parade.

At the bottom of the street, orange sawhorses blocked cars from entering the avenue. Kelly reached for Mrs. B's hand as they turned right toward the church.

Mrs. B would miss St. Mary's so terribly if it was gone. But she couldn't think about that now. She didn't want to think about it at all.

"What's that?" Kelly asked, pointing to the wooden platform.

"That's the judges' stand."

"What are they judging?"

Mrs. B thought for a second. "That's a good question. It's not that big a parade. I guess the best marching unit, best school band. Things like that."

Kelly ran ahead, came back and said, "Mrs. B?"

Mrs. B looked down at the little girl's upturned face.

Kelly said, "You talk to me like I'm an actual person."

"You are an actual person," Mrs. B said.

When they got to the drug store, Mrs. B asked out loud, "Now where should we stand? How about here?" An iron gate was pulled over the front doors but there was still just enough of a recess to block the cold air. The two of them stopped and stood in the doorway.

On the front porch of a house across the street were three children, each a year or two older than the other. Siblings. Must be the Mancini grandkids. Kelly waved to one of the children. The littlest one waved back, then told the next oldest, who turned and waved too.

The boom of a bass drum echoed from far around the bend at the top of the avenue. While folks were rustling about to take their places along the curb, a woman stood up on the porch and walked across the street, a young child in tow. Peggy Regan had been a grade behind Helen. Peggy married Bobby Mancini right out of high school.

"Mrs. B! Haven't seen you in forever. Do you want to come sit on our porch?"

Mrs. B glanced at Kelly, who was looking at the little girl. "Thank you. That would be nice." She took Kelly's hand as they started across the street. "Are these your grandkids?"

Peggy said, "Yep, they're Sheila's girls. She dropped them off and I have them all night. Who is your little one?"

Mrs. B looked down at her charge. "This is Kelly. Kelly, this is Mrs. Mancini."

"Hi," Kelly said.

"Kelly is Laverne Grey's niece. Great-niece, I mean. They moved into Laverne's house when Laverne left for Florida."

"Oh, yeah, somebody told me she moved."

In front of the house, the two other children had already run to meet them. Mrs. B looked down and realized she was still holding Kelly's hand. "You can go play. I'll talk to Mrs. Mancini." Mrs. B climbed the four steps to the porch, holding carefully to the railing. Kelly and the children were already chattering away on the sidewalk.

Peggy said, "I'm making hot chocolate. Here, have a seat. I'll get you a cup."

There was a kitchen chair on the porch, pointed toward the top of the avenue. Mrs. B sat in it. It was still a little warm from when the other woman was sitting there.

Peggy came outdoors with an afghan. "Here you go, Mrs. B." Mrs. B thanked her and put it over her lap. The parade was about to round the bend. They could hear more drums now, and some off-key horns.

Peggy went into the house and got a second kitchen chair. She set it near Mrs. B's, angling it toward the top of the avenue. A third trip into the house yielded two steaming white mugs, each with a Santa decal on the front and a peppermint stick peeking out of the top.

"Hot chocolate."

Mrs. B thanked her. She held the warm mug in her blue gloves and blew on the top. Foam covered the bottom of the peppermint stick.

A white car rounded the bend. The windows were down and a man in a navy suit waved at the crowd from the passenger seat. Peggy said, "Look, here comes the mayor! We're so lucky to have the mayor come every year to our parade."

Mrs. B didn't think much of this mayor. Too much attention to media coverage, too little attention to putting in a hard day's work. "He has a lot of voters in Burchfield," she said. He knows where his bread is buttered, she thought.

Peggy sat back in her puffy black coat and took a sip from her Santa mug, then pulled out the peppermint stick and licked off the foam.

A couple dozen boy scouts marched behind the mayor, doing a pretty good job of staying in formation. Behind them was a group of littler boys. Two of them held a banner that said Burchfield PeeWee Football. The boys weren't in step but they made up for it in confidence. They chanted proudly, "We are Burchfield men, we are football men!"

The next car, a red convertible, was flanked by two tellers from the bank—the two nice ones.

"Don't see Tammy Bartlow," Peggy said. "Guess that's no surprise."

Mrs. B nodded.

The young women wore red wool coats and white hats, with black gloves to match their black boots. A pretty girl, also dressed in red, waved from the car's passenger seat. There were loud cheers from the crowd as she went by.

Peggy stood up. "Wow, it's her! You know, not the one from *American Idol*, the other one."

Even Mrs. B was impressed. "I read somewhere that her dad and Danny McCoy are good friends. They raise money together for some Catholic organization, I forget which. I bet Danny got her to come," Mrs. B said.

The tellers tossed lollipops to the onlookers, and Kelly and the girls scrambled to catch them.

Peggy sat back in her chair. "Boy, he's one for the charities, that Danny is. Catholic Youth Organization, St. Mary's. He might have moved to Chicago to coach the Bears, but he's still a Burchfield kid. You know he paid for all that new gym equipment at the school."

Mrs. B nodded. "He's a good boy."

"He remembers where he came from," Peggy said.

A high school band was next, belting out "Jingle Bells" with plenty of enthusiasm and a little bit of talent. The girls behind them in the marching unit wore sweatsuits topped with feather boas in their school colors. Mrs. B and Peggy looked down at the four children, lined up at the curb. Kelly and the oldest girl were trying to open the lollipops without taking off their mittens. The littlest girl was wiggling to the music.

"That's our Ellie. She loves to dance," Peggy said.

Next came a tall, round snowman, throwing chocolate kisses. Silver wrappers shone under the streetlights as kids ran to fill their pockets. A city councilman walked next to the snowman. Both wore identical black top hats and green striped scarves.

Mrs. B finished her hot chocolate and set the cup on the porch's cement floor. Another marching band came by, playing "Frosty the Snowman." Its majorettes were dressed in white sweatsuits with blue trim.

"They're good," Mrs. B said as a girl jumped and caught a baton, its white streamers glittering under the streetlights.

There was a break in the action after the marching band. To let the rest of the parade catch up, the band marched in place in front of the drugstore. The pause gave the majorettes a chance to show off, and they took advantage of it. The crowd cheered the girls when they moved on.

"Hey, Dan! Danny!" The excitement in the crowd was palpable as a red convertible slowly made its way around the bend and down the avenue. "Danny, over here!"

Danny McCoy was sitting on the back of the convertible with his feet on the black leather seat, beaming and waving at the crowd. His wife, a former beauty queen, was in the front seat, smiling and saying something to the driver. A bunch of cashiers from the supermarket flanked the car, dressed in Chicago Bears football jerseys.

Behind them all was Santa Claus, atop a big red fire engine. Teenage girls in green elf costumes threw candy canes to the crowd. You could hardly hear yourself for the cheering.

"Be hard to tell if this commotion was for Danny or for Santa," Peggy said.

Mrs. B looked to the curb and saw the four little girls waving and jumping up and down. She nodded her head toward them and said, "They're cheering for Santa, that's for sure."

27

As Mrs. B and Kelly tried to make their way through the crowd across from the church, Kelly plowed into the back of a man in a brown corduroy jacket. He turned around. It was Father Sean.

Mrs. B's mouth fell open. He was the last person she expected to see.

Kelly looked up at the young priest and said, "Sorry." She reached out her hands. They were full of the candy she was trying to stuff into her pockets. "Want some?"

Father Sean laughed and patted her on the head. "No, thank you. No harm done." He turned to Mrs. B. "Is this your granddaughter, Mrs. B?"

"No, just a neighbor. Kelly, say hello to Father." Mrs. B tried to act like everything was normal, even though her heart was pounding.

"Hello, Kelly. What a great Irish name. I'm Father Sean." He bent down to shake the little girl's hand. Kelly didn't seem to understand the gesture and handed him a chocolate kiss. He thanked her and began to unwrap it as he turned back to Mrs. B.

Mrs. B recovered enough to say, "I was sorry to hear about your aunt."

"Thank you. She had been sick for a while. I was more worried about my mother. They lived together. By the time I left she seemed okay, though. As well as she could be, anyhow, under the circumstances."

Mrs. B felt a twinge of conscience. "It's never easy to deal with death. But it's a part of life."

"God gives and God takes away," Father said as he put the candy in his mouth.

As they turned toward home, Kelly said, "He talks funny."

Mrs. B took Kelly's hand to cross the street. She was still a little rattled. "He's from Ireland. That's how they talk there," she said.

28

Sunday's evening news promised a snowstorm, so Mrs. B stayed home from the Senior Center on Monday.

After breakfast, she dug into the freezer and pulled out a roasting chicken. It had been there for a while. Freezer burn on the wings, but still good for soup. She put it in the sink to defrost.

As the day went by, Mrs. B tried to keep busy. She went through her mending, sewed on a couple of buttons, threw away a pair of socks. She diced carrots and celery, boiled noodles for the soup. She watched a movie on television. She read the newspaper. She took a broom to her kitchen floor and ran the sweeper in the living room.

The snow didn't come until Monday evening. It wasn't enough to call a storm—only three inches— but it was enough to keep her home on Tuesday.

Tuesday, Mrs. B did the laundry. She cleaned the bathroom. She took a ham bone from the freezer and put it in a pot with an onion and some dried beans she had soaked the night before.

She finished Monday's crossword and pulled out the stack of magazines she had been saving for a rainy day. In a few hours they were all in her recycling bin.

She went through her cabinet and saw a can of apple pie filling way in the back, so she paged through old cookbooks for ideas and found a recipe for apple spice cake.

By Tuesday night her freezer was packed with plastic containers.

Wednesday morning the streets were almost clear, but not quite. She looked out the window on her front door and watched two girls chase each other, laughing and sliding on the sidewalk in front of the O'Malley's house. Tomorrow, she thought. Better wait one more day, just to be safe.

She poured a cup of coffee and sat in her rocker in the living room. It didn't take long to go through the rest of last night's paper. Not much news. She turned on the TV. The classic movie channel was showing a gangster movie. She hit the button on the remote to flip forward through the channel guide. Gangster movies all day. She turned off the TV and picked up the book she had left on the coffee table the night before. After a few minutes, she put that down too.

I've got cabin fever, she thought.

When the mail came, it felt like an event. Mrs. B had her front door open before the mailman left the porch.

A water bill. A circular from the supermarket. Her news magazine.

Then she saw it—a sheet of paper in the mailbox, underneath the mail. It was white with large black letters and said: LEAVE IT ALONE.

Mrs. B sat in her rocker with the stack of mail in her lap, staring at the message. Was this intended for her? What on earth would someone want her to leave alone?

It was almost a minute before it came to her. The church money.

Myrtle, God bless her. She did like to talk. By now she might have told everyone in town that Mrs. B was going to help exonerate her son. But why would anyone listen? How could anyone see an old lady like Mrs. B as a threat?

She looked the message over, but its appearance was very ordinary. A white piece of paper. She held it up to the light. No watermarks, but then you seldom see watermarks anymore. The printing was in black block letters. She ran her fingers over the words. They weren't raised like typewriter letters would be.

Someone printed the sheet on a computer. Anybody could have done it. For goodness sake, Mrs. B probably could have done it if she'd had a little tutoring. She crumpled the paper up, more to make a statement than for any other reason, and threw it in the trash.

In equal amounts Mrs. B was angry and curious. All her life she'd had a dim view of cowards, and an anonymous note was the most cowardly thing she could think of. That a coward would target her, no matter how stupidly, really had her riled. Disdainful, that was the word. That's what she felt. Disdain.

The curiosity was from the message itself. The words "leave it alone" didn't tell her much, but they did say one thing loud and clear. Ron didn't take that money. Someone was afraid of being found out.

29

On Wednesday afternoon, Mrs. B read her news magazine. Problems in Africa, problems in the Middle East. Problems, problems, problems. The European news led with an article about the IRA. Most of it was historical, with a timeline of The Troubles in a green and white graphic at the top of the page.

She sat back and read it carefully. It was interesting, but she didn't learn anything she didn't already know. There was an unnecessarily graphic description of Bloody Sunday in the middle of the article. She read that carefully too, even though she found it distasteful.

The last page of the piece held a listing of the splinter groups she had read about. The information had been compiled with input from Britain's military intelligence unit, MI5. There was a flashy "where are they now?" look to the page, but the pertinent details were listed factually: the name of the group, its year of origin, perceived intentions, known members, known terrorist activities, arrests and convictions. She ran quickly down the list and found Ireland's Liberators.

Father Sean Flaherty was being held in Portlaoise Prison awaiting trial.

She read it again, to be sure she was right, then sat back in her rocker. No one had anything to fear from her. She was a foolish old lady.

30

As the day went on, Mrs. B's embarrassment and self-pity gave way to curiosity and finally full-blown indignance. How dare someone send her an anonymous note? How dare someone try to threaten her?

So Father Sean wasn't a terrorist. So she made a mistake. That didn't mean she had to give up. Ron Monaghan didn't take that money from the church. The person who sent that note did.

An anonymous note, put in a mailbox to scare an old woman. Mrs. B was looking for a low-life, cowardly thief.

Or, she realized suddenly, someone who loved a thief, and wanted to protect them.

When Jeopardy was over that evening, Mrs. B went to her junk drawer and took out a pad of paper with flowers on it and a #2 pencil.

She sat down at the kitchen table and made two columns: *Motive* and *Opportunity*.

Then she put the pencil down again.

Everything Mrs. B knew about detectives was from movies and mystery books. Real detectives couldn't possibly make lists. On television they pasted pictures and drew circles and arrows on big white boards.

She turned over to a new sheet of paper. Maybe it was a logic puzzle.

Okay. Whoever put that message in her mailbox either took the money from the church, or they wanted to protect the person who took the money. What else?

It had to be someone who knew Mrs. B had told Myrtle she'd help find out who stole the money. Who, for sure, knew about her conversation with Myrtle?

She started a new list. Rose and Anne. Old Mike.

Mike found out from an usher at church. How did the usher find out?

If the usher was an older man, he might know Myrtle. If he was a younger man, he might know Ron. Maybe he and Ron laughed about it over a beer at the Grill.

That would mean anyone in the bar could know. Which meant anyone in the neighborhood could know.

She went back to the first sheet of paper and stared at the *Motive* column. Who did she know who might want or need a lot of money?

Don. At computer class he said he wanted to take his wife to Paris for their 50th anniversary. How could he possibly afford that? Don and his wife lived on social security and Don's pension from the mill. Their son brought them groceries when he came to visit. Even if they were frugal, it would take a long time to save enough money to go to Paris.

Mrs. B stood up, walked to the kitchen counter and poured a little clump of raisins from the old spaghetti sauce jar into the palm of her hand, still lost in thought.

Maybe they weren't frugal. Maybe they were spendthrifts and that was why Gregory brought them groceries.

She sat back down again, picked up her pencil and chewed the raisins, staring at the columns.

Opportunity. Rose is in Father Clancy's office all the time.

Though she couldn't think of any reason Rose would want to steal money, Mrs. B did think it was odd that she knew next to nothing about Rose, other than that her husband and son were on the police force.

It had always seemed strange that Rose would never talk about her life before she got married. None of the ladies at their table asked Rose personal questions anymore. She had never given more than the slightest hint of where she was from or what her life was like before she came to Burchfield.

Mrs. B had always supposed Rose was reticent by nature. Maybe that wasn't the case at all. Rose could have a secret that compelled her to need money. Maybe she was being blackmailed over the past she would never talk about.

Do people still blackmail people? Or is that just in old movies?

Rose certainly had access to Father's office. And his keys.

Mrs. B looked down at the paper. On one hand, it seemed ridiculous to suspect Don and Rose. Especially Rose. At least Don got on her nerves sometimes. But if this was a logic puzzle, she couldn't let emotion get in her way. Don might have a motive.

Rose might have a motive and she certainly had opportunity.

Mrs. B got up and put her pajamas on, then sat back down at the table in her robe and slippers. A new thought had occurred to her.

What about Tammy Bartlow? Her customer service was atrocious, but she did seem to know the particulars of her job. She probably knew how to manipulate a bank account.

When Mrs. B was working as a bookkeeper, she could have stolen money from the company by adding a false employee to the payroll. Of course she never would have done anything dishonest—she never even brought home a pencil—but it would have been easy to do. There was a story like that in the paper just last month, about a law firm downtown. It happened all the time.

Any teller could steal from a bank. A smart teller would know how to take money and make it look like someone else did it.

She wrote "Tammy Bartlow" in the *Opportunity* column.

Then she remembered the story Father Clancy told Myrtle about his argument in the bank. She flipped the pencil over and erased Tammy from the column. She'd forgotten the missing money was in a cashier's check in Father's desk.

A cashier's check. Wasn't Michele late picking up Kelly one night because someone cashed a large check at the casino and bought everyone drinks?

Maybe one of Michele's boyfriends stole the money.

Michele went out with quite a few young men. Mrs. B didn't begrudge her that. It was natural for a single mother to be looking for a husband, and any sensible woman would play the field until she was sure about a man. But the men Michele dated weren't the type of men Mrs. B would have chosen for her. They seemed a little flashy, a little loud. She didn't want to use the word unsavory, but they didn't look like marriage material. That one fellow brought her home on a motorcycle. At this time of year! What if it had started to snow?

Mrs. B hadn't recognized any of the men she'd seen with Michele, but they could be from the neighborhood. If they drank at the Grill, they could have heard about Mrs. B promising to help Myrtle. They could have known about the check in Father Clancy's desk.

But did any of that really mean anything? What about motive or opportunity? If she was going to be logical, Mrs. B couldn't put people on her list because she didn't like the way they looked.

What about the men who stood outside on the corner in front of the Grill? They certainly must need money. They didn't seem to work. Maybe one of them heard Father Clancy argue with Tammy Bartlow at the bank.

Mrs. B didn't know the names of the men who loafed on the corner outside the bar day after day, but she knew their faces from the neighborhood. Since a few of them called her by name, she probably knew them when they were boys. They might have been in Little League with Leo, or maybe they went to school at St. Mary's years ago.

Though she never saw the men at Mass, that didn't mean they were bad people. They might be Protestant. They might be Catholic boys who went to a different church. They might be nice boys who were down on their luck.

Then again, those boys were there all day. No job unless they all worked night turn, which seemed unlikely. They could be up to no good. Mrs. B wrote "men who loaf outside bar" in the *Motive* column.

And then in the *Opportunity* column. If the men in the bar spent any time at all with Father Clancy, they knew how trusting he was. Any one of them could have talked his way into Father's office. Or walked by to see if a window or door was open. One of them could have followed Father, maybe even right after he left the bank. It might have been that simple.

Well, in that case, there was no reason Don couldn't walk into Father's office. Any old excuse would have gotten him in. She put his name in the opportunity column.

Mrs. B looked the list over. She didn't have a motive for Tammy, but anyone who is that unpleasant to other people must have a lot of problems. Maybe those included money problems.

After a few seconds of deliberation, she wrote "Tammy Bartlow" in the motive column. It wasn't entirely logical, but it did give her a bit of satisfaction.

31

On a Thursday early in December, it was Mrs. B's turn for kitchen duty. While she washed a platter, Rose stood patiently beside her, dishtowel in hand.

"Don't you love how warm it is over here by the dishwasher? I could stand here all day. My face was frozen when I got here," Rose said.

"It was cold this morning. We don't get those snows, though, like we used to when we were kids," Mrs. B said as she handed the platter to her friend. "Remember, we'd stay home from school two, three days sometimes." She wrung out the dishcloth in the sink. "Boy, I missed my friends when that happened. My favorite friends from school lived blocks away."

"I used to miss my teachers," said Rose as she gave the platter a final swipe and placed it on a shelf. "I had nice teachers. They were strict but when you did something right they gave you a big smile and you felt good all the way home."

Rose was talking about school! How could Mrs. B encourage her? After a few seconds she said, "Spelling bees. Remember the spelling bees?"

"Every Friday morning. They would line you up along the blackboard," Rose said.

"Us too," Mrs. B said. "You had to know all the spelling words from that week."

"I bet you did good at that, Edwina." Rose was bent over with a butter knife in her hand, scraping cheese off the door of the stove. When Mrs. B turned to reply, all she could see was the puckered waistband of Rose's royal blue slacks and the bottom of her sweatshirt.

"Spelling was one of my best subjects," Mrs. B said. "I had to sit down early one time, though, because I forgot to repeat the word before I spelled it. It was an easy word, too."

"My hard words were always the ones with i-e in it." Rose gave a satisfied grunt, turned around and put a handful of cheese crumbles in the trashcan. "I could never figure out if it was i-e or e-i."

"I still have to think about that sometimes. That rhyme they teach you, that 'i before e except after c,' it doesn't always work," Mrs. B said. As she wiped down the counter she wondered if she should venture another question. She decided to try. "Did you have nuns for teachers?"

"My favorite teacher was Miss Benjamin in the fourth grade," Rose said. "I liked almost all of my teachers but she was the best. I used to stay after school with her and clap erasers, and we would talk about everything, just the two of us. She was so nice to me."

Rose wiped her hands on her apron, folded it and put it in the drawer beside the silverware. "Well, that's done. I better get going. I've got a roast thawing out in my sink. See you tomorrow, Ed."

32

Mrs. B made her way back to the lunch table to pull her heavy blue coat off the back of her chair. When she tied the babushka under her chin, she could smell dish soap on her hands.

She had just picked up her purse and hung it on her arm when she spotted Myrtle and Anne across the room. Their heads were bent together and they were talking quietly. Anne looked concerned.

Mrs. B walked toward them, and the three women headed toward the door. After a few steps, Myrtle stopped suddenly. Mrs. B and Anne turned to look at her.

Myrtle's face was scrunched and she looked like she was going to cry. "Did my Ronnie take that money? He didn't have his lying face but now he's a grown man and maybe I can't tell. Maybe he learned how to lie. Maybe he took that money and he has to go to jail." She looked down at her shoes. "I don't want to think my Ronnie is bad, but what if he is? What if he really is?"

Mrs. B and Anne both stood closer to her. Mrs. B took both of Myrtle's hands in hers.

"Now you listen to me, Myrtle," Mrs. B said. "I don't know what happened to that money, but I know your Ronnie didn't take it."

Myrtle looked at her, wide-eyed. "How do you know?" She sniffled and started digging through her pockets.

The three of them were the last ones in the room. Father Sean was standing politely at the door, waiting for them to leave so he could lock up. The women walked outside and when they were out of earshot Mrs. B said, "Ron didn't take that money, Myrtle. I can't prove it yet, but I know he didn't take it."

Anne gave Mrs. B a searching look, then turned to Myrtle and said, "Now don't you worry. Worrying doesn't help anything."

"Okay," Myrtle said. "I'm not going to worry. I'm glad it wasn't my Ronnie. I'm glad he's a good boy.

I'll try not to worry. And if I get scared, I'll just say Ed will fix it. That will calm me down." She pulled a torn tissue from the pocket of her tan jacket. "And then I'll say a rosary."

"Definitely, say a rosary," Mrs. B said. "Ask the Blessed Mother. I'm sure she was worried about her Son all the time."

"Do you really think so?" Myrtle put the crumpled tissue back in her pocket and wiped her eyes with the back of a red mitten.

Anne said, "Of course she worried about Him. He's supposed to be home building cabinets and instead He's out traipsing all over creation with a bunch of fishermen."

33

When Mrs. B turned to the left to walk up the avenue, Anne turned with her.

"Didn't you drive today?" Mrs. B asked.

"I didn't walk on the treadmill yesterday. I figured if I walked to the Senior Center and back, that would catch me up on my exercise. I have to stop at Lefty Cameron's office anyhow to pay my insurance," Anne said. "Where are you headed?"

"Tony's. I'm almost out of milk," Mrs. B said as they crossed the street. When the ladies reached the corner, a young man left the Grill and the dank sweet smell of barroom wafted through the open door. The ladies both glanced in. The back of a booth blocked their vision, but they could clearly see Father Clancy talking intently to someone across from him.

"Father's getting an early start," Anne said.

"Maybe he's ministering to someone," Mrs. B said. Anne made a face and they both started to giggle.

When they reached the doorway to Tony's store, Anne said, "I'll walk in with you. I'm not in any hurry."

Anne and Mrs. B were the only two in the store. Mrs. B went to the refrigerator case and pulled out a plastic bottle of 2% milk. She took it to the counter just as Patrick was coming out of the back. As he rang her up, Anne said, "Was it true what you said to Myrtle? About Ronnie, I mean."

Mrs. B dug through her purse to give Patrick the exact change. "It is."

"How do you know?"

Mrs. B paused and then turned to her friend. "You know, Anne, I don't want to sound mysterious, but I'd rather keep the reason to myself for now. I'll tell you as soon as I feel comfortable. But I do know."

"Okay," Anne said. "Now I'm going to be on pins and needles until you tell me. I'll have to find something to occupy myself in the meantime." She looked over the candy rack below the counter, reached for a chocolate bar and began to count out change. "This will have to do me."

As the two ladies departed, Mrs. B glanced back and saw Patrick standing quietly at the counter, watching them walk away.

Outside, Mrs. B said goodbye to Anne and turned toward home just as Ron Monaghan came out of the bar. She opened her mouth to greet him but he was on the other side of the avenue before she could even say hello. His head was down and his hands were in his pockets. He looked like he was carrying the weight of the world.

34

Mrs. B pulled a chicken pot pie from its cardboard box and then remembered her coffee cup was still in the living room. When she reached for it on the TV table near her rocker, she saw Kelly's face bouncing up and down in the window of the front door.

"I was knocking. Didn't you hear me?" The girl was standing on the little step in the doorway, reaching into Mrs. B's mailbox.

"I was in the kitchen," Mrs. B said as she stepped aside to let Kelly in.

"I came to see you. It's boring at my house." Mrs. B took the little stack of mail into the kitchen and set it on the table. Kelly shrugged off her coat and tagged along behind her. Opening the freezer, Mrs. B pulled out a second pot pie and began to read the directions on the back of the box.

Kelly sat at the kitchen table. "What are you making?"

"Pot pie."

"I like pot pie."

Mrs. B nodded. "I thought you might."

Kelly reached toward the stack of papers on the table. "Do you want me to open your mail?"

"No. Mail is private. You can read me who they're from, though."

Kelly picked up the stack and stared at the top envelope. Mrs. B glanced over at her from the microwave. "It's in the top corner."

Kelly pulled out a circular from the bottom of the pile. "This one's from the supermarket." Then a green envelope. "This is from Parkside Bank."

Mrs. B punched numbers into the microwave, then looked over at Kelly again. As the machine began to hum, Kelly held the green envelope in the air for Mrs. B to see. "That's just an advertisement," Mrs. B said. "What else is there?"

Kelly pulled out another circular and a white piece of paper slid out from underneath. In big, bold letters it said, "Leave it alone." Kelly read it aloud.

Mrs. B had the coffee pot in her hand, and she set it down with a thud. She walked over to Kelly and snatched the piece of paper from her hand. With a grimace, she crumpled it and threw it in the garbage can by the back door.

"What was that, Mrs. B?" Kelly asked. Her voice was shaky.

Mrs. B stopped in her tracks. The poor child wouldn't have thought a thing about that note if she hadn't gotten angry. "Ignore it," she said, but the words came out more gruffly than she intended. She forced herself to soften her tone. "What do you want to drink?"

"Orange juice." Kelly rifled through the rest of the mail two or three times, not looking up. Finally she said, "Mrs. B, did a bad person send you that?"

"Don't worry about it." Mrs. B could hear the edge in her own voice, and when she looked at Kelly's face she saw how she was upsetting the girl. She felt terrible.

Kelly watched Mrs. B pour the orange juice. Then she said timidly, "Did everybody on our street get one of those?"

Mrs. B put the glass in front of Kelly. Protectiveness overcame her anger, and when her words came out they sounded comforting. "You don't need to be scared. I'm sure I'm the only person that came to."

She patted the little girl's hair. "It really is nothing to worry about. I got one before and absolutely nothing happened. So you don't even need to think about it."

Kelly's eyes were wide. "Are you sure?"

"Yes, I'm sure. There's no reason for you to be afraid."

Kelly pondered this for a minute. "You should get a dog, Mrs. B. Then if a bad person came the dog could bite them."

The microwave beeped four times. Mrs. B reached for a potholder, saying, "I don't want a dog."

Kelly was undaunted. "If you got a dog I could walk it for you. I would only charge you a dollar a day."

Mrs. B burst into laughter. "So if I don't get a dog, I save $365 a year? I could buy a lot of pot pies with that. I think I'll take my chances."

35

After they ate, Mrs. B played a game of dominoes with Kelly and then they watched sitcom reruns. Partway into the second show, Mrs. B's mind began to wander. She remembered she needed to get peanut butter at the grocery store, which reminded her she had to take Helen's package to the post office, which reminded her she hadn't yet invited Michele and Kelly for Christmas. If memory served, Emily Post recommended two weeks to a month prior for a holiday dinner invitation.

She let Kelly change the channel to a children's show, then got up from her rocker and went to the bedroom. From her dresser drawer, she pulled out a stationery set. She thumbed through a few notecards before she found the perfect one. It was trimmed in red and green and had a snowman on the front. She sat at the kitchen table and began to write.

Michele,
I would very much like it if you and Kelly would join me for Christmas dinner. Please let me know whether you can come. I look forward to hearing from you.
Mrs. B

Mrs. B stared at it for a minute, then realized she was chewing on the end of her pen. Her stomach was full of butterflies. She felt like a teenager getting ready for a date.

She had been counting on spending Christmas with Kelly and Michele. For the first time she realized it was very possible they would have other plans.

How could she not have considered that before? Of course they would have plans. They had family nearby. Christmas is spent with family. Not with an old lady across the street you just met a couple of months ago.

Mrs. B allowed herself a full minute of self-pity, then realized she had slumped in her chair and forced herself to sit up straight. Oh, well. Nothing ventured, nothing gained. She licked the envelope and sealed it, then walked to the living room and put it on the couch on top of Kelly's coat.

Kelly had the remote and was flipping through the channels. "What's that?"

"It's a note for your mom."

"What's it say?"

"It's an invitation. I asked her if you two can come over here on Christmas."

Kelly tossed the remote onto the coffee table and put on her coat.

"Where are you going?" Mrs. B asked.

"I have to put it on my mom's dresser. Bye, Mrs. B."

Mrs. B let her out, then picked up the crossword puzzle and her #2 pencil. Three more words. Sometimes when she set the crossword down for a few hours and picked it up again, the answers came easily. This was one of those days. She was filling the last letters into the little numbered blocks when the phone rang.

It was Michele. "Hi, Mrs. B. Kelly brought me your note."

"She ran out of here rather quickly." Mrs. B felt those butterflies again. She could hear Kelly chattering in the background.

"She really wants us to come," Michele said. "What time were you going to eat? We're going over Anthony's, but they won't eat until about six because Anthony's working daylight. I'm working Christmas Eve so I got the whole day off."

Mrs. B had been so nervous writing the invitation she'd forgotten to include the time. She gave a sigh of relief and her face broke into a grin. "I like to eat at noon on Christmas. Can you come over then?"

"Sure. If I forget, Kelly will remind me."

Mrs. B placed the phone in the receiver, then walked to the kitchen and turned on the radio. Christmas carols. She sang along as she went through her cupboard to double-check she had everything she needed to make the ham.

36

On Sunday morning, wind stung Mrs. B's nose while she walked to church. When she got there, the wind had died down some and Rose was standing outside on the broad sidewalk. Her son Bobby was having a heated discussion with Ron Monaghan. Mrs. B went over to say hello and, though she would have been embarrassed to admit it, to find out what they were arguing about.

"Hi, Rose."

"Hi, Ed."

The two women stood together for a minute, listening to the men argue. It wasn't anything interesting. They were bickering about a call the referee made at the Bears game last Sunday.

"I don't know why I'm waiting for him," Rose said finally. Someone opened the church door, and they could hear the first hymn starting.

Rose said, "Bobby, I'm going in."

"I'm coming, Mom." He turned back to Ron. "Ronnie, you're nuts. That's all I can say about it. You need your head examined." The two men walked in together, genuflecting in the aisle before taking their respective places in the pews.

Mrs. B sang quietly to the hymn, all the while wondering what to make for dessert after Christmas dinner. She debated the merits of various pies and cakes. By the time they sat down for the sermon, she had decided on chocolate chip cookies.

When Father Clancy got to the pulpit, he began the announcements with the news that there would be a second collection at the request of Father Sean. The money would go to Trócaire, an Irish charity that sends mercy missions to places in need.

Mrs. B sheepishly pulled a dollar out of her purse and stuck it in her pocket for the collection plate.

37

Mrs. B took two sweaters out of the chifforobe and laid them next to each other on her cream-and-lavender bedspread. One was a green pullover with gold beaded snowflakes, the other a red cardigan with snowman buttons and smiling snowmen on the pockets. She put a pair of black slacks between them and stood for a few minutes looking back and forth between the two.

Then she remembered Anne said she was going to wear a green sweater. Mrs. B reached for the cardigan, put it on over her pajama top, and looked in the mirror.

Yes.

She reached under her bed and pulled out her black shoes with the bow on the front. She put the other sweater away and pulled out a pair of silky black trouser socks. Then she set the outfit together on the bed and stepped back to look at it.

Yes.

She went to the kitchen to get the coffee started, then sat down to work the crossword. The Christmas party at the Senior Center wouldn't start until eleven o'clock. Sister Wilhelmina and the other retired nuns were doing the decorating, and if it was anything like last year they would be working up until the last minute.

Mrs. B had two cups of coffee, finished the crossword. Still, by ten thirty she was dressed and rummaging through her jewelry box, looking for something to accent the outfit. The black beads would match, and the black bow for her hair. She held each of them up to the mirror, then put them both back and pulled out a snowman pin with green eyes. She attached it to the shoulder of her sweater and walked over to the mirror. Then she looked at her face and picked up a comb to fix her bangs.

38

When the door to the Senior Center shut behind her, Mrs. B stood for a second, taking in the view.

The lunch tables had been placed in long rows and covered with red paper tablecloths. Poinsettias in foil-covered pots sat at intervals along the tables. A large nativity scene stood at the far end of the hall, next to a Christmas tree decorated in red and gold.

It was beautiful.

Anne and Rose had already arrived and were saving her a seat at the table farthest from the door. Mrs. B walked through the hubbub of conversations and made her way toward them.

"The sisters did a nice job, didn't they?" Rose said.

"They certainly did," Mrs. B said. Anne and Rose had hung their coats on the backs of their chairs and their scarves on the chairs across the table. They were still standing, taking it all in.

"Did you see the Christmas ornaments? They're the ones we made in crafts class," Anne said as she headed toward the tree. Rose and Mrs. B followed. The tree was next to the coffee station, which looked the same but was next to a table filled with cookies. On the kitchen counter was a large sheet cake. Three nuns were bustling about in the kitchen, and the smell of turkey wafted through the doorway.

The big green plastic tree looked almost real until you got up close. It was covered in gold bulbs and red felt poinsettias. A tall, wispy angel stood on top. "There's lights but they don't have them turned on," Rose said as she reached through a branch. "They must be waiting for everybody to get here first."

Mrs. B was admiring the nativity scene. "They have the baby in the manger already. We never put him there until Christmas day."

"I expect they didn't know where to put him," Anne said as she looked at the large plastic figures. "He wasn't going to fit under Mary's dress."

Myrtle giggled. She had come up behind them, still in her coat. "It took me forever to get dressed. I put on three outfits. Wow, it's so pretty in here! Did you see all the cookies?"

Just then, Sister Wilhelmina came onto the little stage at the end of the room and tapped on a microphone. "Will you all take your seats, please?" Her voice had an authoritative air, and there was a shuffle as the seniors complied. "Father is ready to say grace." Father Clancy stood to her right, a few deferential steps behind her.

"Ooh, let's sit down," Rose said. Myrtle followed them to the table and took the seat they'd saved her, next to Mrs. B. Old Mike was in the seat on the other side of Mrs. B. He nodded hello as the ladies sat.

Father began to speak, and they all bowed their heads. The chatter began again as soon as they all said "Amen." As the sisters came out to serve the meal, Don and Vic took the two empty seats across from Old Mike. Each of them held a mug of coffee. Don was wearing a red ball cap.

Vic said, "What are we having this party now for? It's two weeks till Christmas."

"Shhh," said Anne as one of the nuns approached their table.

"Oh, Sister, the decorations are beautiful!" Rose said as her plate was placed before her.

"We are pleased with the way it turned out this year," Sister said as she took a lunch from her cart and laid it in front of Mrs. B, being careful to serve from the left. "Sister Theresa picked out these green plates. Don't they look pretty on the red tablecloth?"

Mrs. B looked at the shiny plastic plate, covered with turkey, mashed potatoes, glazed carrots and red beet salad. It certainly did look festive.

Father Clancy was walking among the tables, greeting everyone as he went. Eventually he made his way up the aisle toward them.

"Merry Christmas, ladies. Are you enjoying yourselves?"

They all agreed it was a lovely party.

"The Sisters really outdid themselves this time," Father said.

They all agreed.

As Father moved along past them Mrs. B heard him say, "Nice sweater, Vic. Suits you."

Despite herself, Mrs. B turned to look. It *was* a nice sweater, a cream-colored cable knit with dark green collar and cuffs.

Vic looked up at the old priest and nodded. "New. That money from the Bears game."

Father shook his head. "Can't believe our Danny let me down on that one."

"He did right by me," Vic said. "Got this down that Irish store in Station Square. Sale. Regular price was a hundred bucks. Can you picture that? A hundred bucks for a sweater?"

Mrs. B had already turned back to her lunch, but she could hear Don chime in. "My wife thinks a hundred bucks is nothing. I make her show me receipts when she goes to the mall. I don't know where she thinks this money's coming from."

"Stuff costs more now," Vic said. "What, do you want your wife walking around looking like a bum?"

Vic just likes to argue, Mrs. B thought as she turned her attention to her lunch.

Father Clancy left them and continued his walk up and down the aisles between the tables, saying hello to everyone he passed. His manner was jovial, but Mrs. B sensed a melancholy behind it. I bet he's worried about whether the church is going to close, she thought. That must be on his mind all the time.

Anne looked up from her lunch to say, "I was over Tony's the other day picking up a loaf of bread, and I think I smelled marijuana."

Rose said, "Really?"

Vic spoke up. "Probably his kid."

"Patrick?" Mrs. B said.

Don said, "Wouldn't have to be Patrick. That

smell lingers. Could have been somebody walked into the store."

"What do you mean, the smell lingers? What, are you a narcotics agent now?" Vic said.

"I have two sons," Don said with his mouth full. "I remember what that stinky weed smells like." He took another bite of turkey. "Last week I thought I smelled it down the bank."

Vic said, "Somebody ought to give some wacky weed to that teller, that redhead down the end. The mean one. They ought to give her some kind of tranquilizer."

Everyone knew who he was talking about. Don said, "We used to know her mother. Remember her, Vic?"

"Who?"

"Shirley Bartlow," Don said. "The broad handed out the paychecks down the mill."

"Yeah, she was a bitch, too," Vic said.

Sister Wilhelmina stepped back to the microphone.

"Oh, look!" whispered Myrtle. She tapped Mrs. B on the shoulder and pointed toward the door.

A gray-haired woman in a corduroy jumper was standing just inside the Senior Center's entrance. With her were about twenty children, all busily piling their coats and hats onto three nearby chairs.

Sister Wilhelmina said, "While the sisters are cutting the cake and getting ready to serve dessert, we have a special treat for you. Mrs. Walsh's second grade class is here, and they have been practicing a special choral performance for your enjoyment."

The students walked in double-file, their teacher in the lead. When they reached the stage, the children formed three rows, the taller students behind the shorter ones. The girls all wore navy skirts and white blouses, and some of the girls had red ribbons in their hair. The boys wore navy slacks, white shirts and navy ties. They all looked happy to be away from the classroom.

When they were in formation, Mrs. Walsh pulled a round silver pitch pipe from her pocket and blew into it. She raised her arms dramatically, and the students burst into song. "We WISH you a merry Christmas, we WISH you a merry Christmas . . . ."

Mrs. B turned her chair a little to see better. What the children didn't have in musical ability they made up for in energy and charm. They finished the first song, then launched into what was obviously their favorite, "Rudolph the Red-Nosed Reindeer." Mrs. Walsh put on a pair of felt antlers as they began, to the obvious delight of her students.

As they sang, "He'll go down in HIS-to-RY," Mrs. B turned to look around the room. Every senior was paying rapt attention. Other than the singing, you could have heard a pin drop. Even the nuns in the kitchen had come to the doorway, their faces beaming.

After the last note, Mrs. Walsh announced, "We have one more song for you, but first . . . Sisters?"

One nun left the kitchen and went to the Christmas tree, and another went to the doorway. The lights went out, leaving only a little haze of brightness from the glass block windows. And then the tree exploded in sparkling white lights. As everyone oohed and aahed, the children began "Silent Night."

There was a respectful silence afterward, followed by applause and laughter as the lights went on. The children took a bow, then lined up double-file and followed their teacher to the door.

"Oh, that was so beautiful!" Myrtle said as they watched the kids scramble into their coats. "Sometimes I forget what Christmas is about but 'Silent Night' always makes me remember."

"We used to sing it in German at our house," Anne said. "Then the next morning we got our orange and our candy bar."

"We always got an orange too!" Myrtle said. "Wonder why they always gave us oranges?"

"I expect it was a special treat. Eating an orange in the middle of winter," Mrs. B said.

"And eating a whole candy bar by yourself, not having to share it with your brothers and sisters," Anne said.

"Ooh! And walnuts!" Myrtle said. "My mother kept the nutcracker in the kitchen drawer, and we were allowed to bring it in the living room on Christmas morning and crack our walnuts in front of the tree." `

Rose, as usual when they reminisced, smiled and nodded but didn't join in. Maybe Rose never got gifts as a child. There were a lot of foster children years ago. Some were treated badly, more like servants than children. Could Rose have been a foster child?

As one of the Sisters came by with cake and coffee, Mrs. B heard Don mention the casino.

"Yeah, I just went down there for the first time. Won $200 on one of them slot machines. Soon as I won, I cashed it in and dragged Mary Ann out of there. She'd stay there all the goddamn day. One time she went down with those girls in that knitting club and she didn't even tell me until after. I told her she shouldn't be loafing with those young girls. I have to watch her like a hawk." Don waved a forkful of cake in the air. "She came home the other day with an extra earring in her ear, up above her regular earring. If she thinks I'm buying her three earrings every time it's our anniversary, she's got a hole in her head." He stopped and laughed. "Not just in her ear."

Mrs. B said, "Laverne Grey's niece works at the casino. Did you see her there? She's a thin girl with long dark hair. Her name's Michele."

"There was a girl bringing around drinks looked like that. She dress like her aunt, a lot of glittery stuff?"

Mrs. B nodded.

Don said, "Yeah, I bet that was her. She probably makes good tips. She was giving a wink and a wiggle to all the guys there. She even started to flirt with me before Mary Ann came over and gave her a look."

They were interrupted by one of the nuns, who was at the microphone on stage. "Before we take the plates away, take a look under yours. If you have a gold star, you get to bring home one of the lovely poinsettia plants donated by Foster's Nursery."

The ladies all checked under their plates, but none of them had won. Don tipped his plate, then flipped it over and stood up.

"Gold star. I guess I'll take this home to Mary Ann. I'll tell her I bought it for her. She won't know the difference." He grabbed a white poinsettia wrapped in red foil and placed it in front of him.

When Mrs. B and her lady friends finished their cake and coffee and got up to put on their coats, Mrs. B said, "Wait for me?" and walked toward the far corner of the room near the stage, where the Chinese ladies were sitting.

"Lily, can you tell me how to say 'Merry Christmas' in Chinese?"

"Shengdan kuaile!" Lily told her.

Mrs. B addressed the ladies. "Sheng dang qui la!"

The ladies all grinned, and two of them said, "Happy holiday!"

"It was a nice party, wasn't it?" Mrs. B said as she put on her gloves.

"Oh, the children sang so nice!" Lily said. "And I won the prize!" She had a red poinsettia plant in front of her, next to her purse.

Mrs. B walked back to join her friends. They stopped in the kitchen to thank the nuns. Then the four of them, laughing and talking together, walked out the door.

<u>39</u>

"**D**id you do that? Sled ride on a shovel?"

Kelly was curled in a ball at the edge of Mrs. B's couch. Mrs. B was in her rocking chair with her feet up on the matching footstool. The two of them were watching *It's a Wonderful Life* on the classic movie channel.

Mrs. B said, "No, I grew up in the city. I did used to slide down the hill to school on my bookbag."

"Boy, I wish I could do that," Kelly said.

"You couldn't do that now," Mrs. B said. "Too many cars."

"Our street's too flat anyhow." Kelly hadn't

moved her eyes from the TV, and now she jumped as a little boy fell into an icy pond.

When he was rescued by his brother, Kelly relaxed and sat back on the couch. She peppered Mrs. B with comments during nearly every scene.

"That girl likes him," Kelly said as a young George Bailey dished out ice cream to a little blonde at a soda fountain. When the girl whispered "I'll love you till the day I die" in the boy's ear, Kelly turned to Mrs. B with a satisfied face and said, "See?"

An old man grabbed George by the shirt and chased him around the counter, beating him until his ear bled. Mrs. B worried that the movie might be too grown-up for Kelly to watch. She started to get up from her rocker, then studied the little girl's face. She was engrossed in the scene.

The old man dropped to his knees and hugged the boy to him. Kelly turned to Mrs. B and said, "He didn't mean to hit him."

Mrs. B decided to leave the movie on and keep a close eye on Kelly.

A pretty girl in a form-fitting dress made a flirty entrance and exit. Men ogled as she walked by. Kelly said, "What's her name?"

"Violet," Mrs. B said.

"She's like my mom," Kelly said.

Oh my, Mrs. B thought, but she didn't say anything.

During a warm family dinner scene, Kelly turned to look at Mrs. B. "That lady's like you, Mrs. B. Except she has black hair." She turned back to the TV. "And you don't have a waitress at your house."

"When it's in your house, the person's called a maid," Mrs. B said.

Kelly watched the dinner scene a little longer, then asked, "Did you used to have a husband?"

Mrs. B was taken aback, but had to admit it was a reasonable question. She said, "Yes, I had a husband."

"What happened to him?"

"He died."

"Was he nice or mean?" Kelly asked.

"Nice," Mrs. B said.

Kelly thought a crowded party scene, full of young people dancing the Charleston, was hilarious. When it ended with them jumping into the water fully clothed, Mrs. B thought Kelly would laugh even harder. Instead she said, "They're gonna get yelled at when they get home."

George and his date shared a phone call with their friend in New York. Just as the scene became romantic, Kelly said, "Why do they all say hee-haw?"

Mrs. B had gotten so engrossed in the movie she'd forgotten for a second Kelly was there. "They only say it to that one man, Sam Wainwright," Mrs. B said.

"Why?" Kelly said.

"Because he says it all the time."

"Why?"

"He thinks it's funny, I guess."

Kelly made a face. "It's stupid."

"Watch the movie," Mrs. B said.

Mrs. B never expected the old movie to hold Kelly's interest, but there was no doubt it did. The little girl kept up her commentary throughout:

"Why did she make him dinner in that haunted house?"

"Boy, they have a lot of kids."

"Is that guy rich? He looks rich."

Halfway through the movie, an intense discussion between George and his Uncle Billy escalated. When the younger man grabbed the older man by the lapels and began to shake him, Kelly jerked back. Quietly, Mrs. B got up from her rocker and went to sit on the couch next to her.

George's mood at home went from sad to despondent. When he picked up his son and held him too tightly, Kelly asked, "Is he drunk?"

"No," Mrs. B said. "He's just worried."

A little while later, George wrecked his car. Kelly said, "Now he's drunk."

Mrs. B had to agree. "Yes, now he is."

Kelly lay down on the couch and put her head on a throw pillow. Mrs. B thought she was falling asleep, but when George jumped into a snowy river Kelly said, "He's gonna catch ammonia."

"Pneumonia," Mrs. B said.

Kelly drifted off soon after. Mrs. B covered her with a rose-and-gold afghan and sat next to her while she watched the rest of the movie. By the time it was over, it was dark outside.

Mrs. B rose from the couch slowly and made her way to the hallway. She looked up Michele's number in the red book she kept by the phone. When Michele didn't answer, Mrs. B left a message. She hated leaving messages.

"Michele? This is Mrs. B. Kelly's on my couch, asleep. I didn't want to wake her." She didn't know what else to say, so she hung up.

She went back to the living room and picked up the newspaper, half-watching the television. After a while Julie Kennedy knocked on the door.

"Hi, Mrs. B. Michele asked me to come get Kelly."

Kelly woke at the sound of Julie's voice. She turned to Mrs. B and said softly, "I fell asleep."

"I noticed that," Mrs. B said.

The little girl wriggled as Julie tried to stuff her arms into the sleeves of her coat. Kelly mumbled, "What happened at the end?"

Mrs. B said, "All his friends came to help him. And then Sam Wainwright saved the day."

"The rich guy?" Kelly asked.

"The one that said hee-haw," Mrs. B said.

"The nice rich guy," Kelly said. Julie was dragging her toward the door, and the little girl seemed like she was struggling to stay awake.

"Yes, the nice rich guy," Mrs. B said.

As Mrs. B opened the front door for the girls, Kelly looked up. "What about the little girl that was playing the piano? Did her dad quit being mean?"

A wave of protectiveness came over Mrs. B. She said, "Everybody was happy at the end. Everybody came to their house and sang a song together."

"The kids, too?" Kelly asked, navigating the step to the porch while holding Julie's hand.

"The kids, too," Mrs. B said.

"Okay." She seemed satisfied.

Julie said, "Bye, Mrs. B."

"Bye."

Mrs. B turned on the porch light, locked the door, and stood at the window until Julie and Kelly were across the street and safely inside. Then she went to the bedroom to change into her pajamas.

40

"Ronnie's getting ready for his trial. I told him he might not have to go. Ed might have it all figured out before then, what happened to that money."

Rose looked at Mrs. B and caught her eye, but didn't say anything. No one at the table did.

Myrtle turned to Anne and Rose. "Father told me he got that cash check and it got stolen. So Ed just has to figure out who took the cash check. She already figured out it wasn't my Ronnie."

"Cashier's check," Mrs. B said.

"Cashier's check," Myrtle said. "You know Father. Maybe he lost it. Maybe he'll find it tomorrow in a book he was reading. Maybe he stuck it in for a bookmark. Maybe nobody even stole it at all."

Anne and Mrs. B tried to smile and nod encouragingly. Rose studied her lunch plate as if she was memorizing it for a test.

"Anyway, I'm not worrying about it. I'm just doing my praying and that's it. I'm not smart enough to fix things. I know that. But Ed and the Blessed Mother will fix things, and everything is going to be fine."

Myrtle settled back in her seat. "Ron bought a suit to wear to the trial. He got too fat for his old one. The coat won't button. It's navy blue. The new suit. It's navy blue."

"A navy suit is always nice. It has a very classic look," Anne said.

Myrtle said, "So I'm not worried. I'm talking to the Blessed Mother, just like you told me. 'Mary,' I say to her, 'Will you talk to your Son? He'll listen to you. Ask him to straighten things out for my Ronnie. He's a good boy. Thank you. In the name of the Father, the Son, and the Holy Spirit, Amen.'" She crossed herself as she finished. "I say that every morning, and every night before I go to bed. And I know she's listening, so I'm just waiting to see what happens. I hope she gets Jesus to fix everything soon.

I don't want to tell her I'm in a hurry or anything, but I don't want Ronnie to have to be on the TV news. Though he will look nice in that suit."

Nobody knew what to say after that. Myrtle finally said, "Is that pumpkin pie?" and everyone spoke up at once.

"Yes," said Rose and Mrs. B at the same time. Anne blurted, "Yes. It's pumpkin."

Myrtle didn't seem to notice. She said, "I think there's whipped cream in the fridge left over from yesterday. I'll go sneak back and look."

As soon as she left the table, the three of them began to talk quietly.

"I don't know what to say," Mrs. B said.

"What is there to say?" Anne said.

Rose paused for a minute, then said, "Bob and Bobby were in the living room last week when I was in the kitchen and I could hear them talking. Bob told Bobby he heard Father took the money out of the bank in a big check, and he was asking Bobby if he knew anything about it. Bobby said it couldn't be true because the money came out in dribs and drabs."

Anne and Mrs. B stared at Rose.

Rose looked down at her pie, then set her fork aside. "I feel so bad for Myrtle. Bobby sat behind

Ronnie all through school. They've known each other forever."

Myrtle came back with a container of whipped topping half-hidden under her arm. She set it on the table and said, "Ta-da! Who wants some?"

Rose pushed her plate forward. So did Anne and Mrs. B.

41

Mrs. B pulled the string at the bottom of the steps and a bare light bulb came to life. She was glad she put her jacket on before she went down to the cellar. It was cold. Cold and damp.

The Christmas decorations were probably on the right, near the old roasting pan. She looked at the shelf above her head. There was the big Christmas tree they had used every year after Albert quit getting them a real one. "You can keep this up longer," he said. Someone from the mill was selling them for half price. "Fell off a truck," Albert said with a wink.

After Helen got married, Leo used to put up the tree for Mrs. B. They would play Christmas carols while they decorated it, and when they were all done, he would reach up and put the angel at the top.

Mrs. B wondered how Leo would spend Christmas. In a shelter, she supposed. She hoped. Her only contact with him over the years had been postcards. Five in all. None said anything but her address, scrawled in Leo's shaky handwriting. She supposed it was his way of telling her he was alive. They all had California postmarks. Every time she got one, she said a novena for his safety. Then she threw the card away.

Mrs. B never used the tree anymore.

She looked on the shelf that was eye level and started rooting through the boxes. She found a ceramic Christmas tree that had the lights built in. She pulled it out. Three boxes later she found her Nativity set. She pulled that out, then the old skater figurines her grandmother brought over from Poland. She held them in her hand for a moment, feeling the warmth of the memories. Then she put them in her pocket and started her search again.

She knew somewhere she had a large picture of Mary and baby Jesus, one that lit up when you plugged it in. It took a while but she finally found it, on the other side of the room by the canned tomatoes. It was wrapped in two shopping bags, one over the bottom and one over the top to keep the dust out.

She stepped back and looked at her stash. She might be able to get everything upstairs in two trips. The water heater banged as she headed up with her first lot.

42

Kelly came over while Mrs. B was decorating. She was just about halfway done. The ceramic tree was on the coffee table, and the table was covered with a white sheet, crumpled up in peaks and valleys to give a semblance of snow. A little mirror lay flat and held the two skaters. The picture was propped on the floor near the television, and Mrs. B was just starting to set up the Nativity set on a little table near her rocker.

"There's a package on your porch," Kelly said.

"It looks like it's in your hands, not on my porch," Mrs. B said as she let her in.

"I brought it in for you," Kelly said. "It's from England. It says so in the corner."

Mrs. B picked it up and looked at it. "It's from my daughter Helen."

"You have kids?" Kelly said.

"I have a daughter and a son."

"How old are they? Where do they live?"

"They're grownups. My son lives in California." That wasn't a lie, not really. As far as she knew, he was in California. "Do you want to guess where my daughter lives?"

"England?" Kelly said as she took off her coat.

"Yes, she lives in London."

"Why do they live so far away?" Kelly asked.

"I wish I knew," Mrs. B said as she pulled Mary and Joseph from their compartments in an old brown cardboard box.

"Aren't you gonna open it?" Kelly said, picking up the package again.

"No, it's for Christmas, I'm sure. Just set it down somewhere."

"Oh, this looks so pretty!" Kelly said when she saw the coffee table. She picked up one of the skater figurines.

Mrs. B turned with a start, then softly and quietly said, "Kelly, please don't touch those. They're very old and they could break easily. Just put it back gently."

Kelly was as careful as could be putting it back down. She walked around to the other side of the coffee table. "Can I plug in the tree?"

"You need an extension cord," Mrs. B said.

"Where's it at?"

"In the kitchen, in the junk drawer. The bottom drawer in the cupboard where the plates are."

In about twenty minutes the decorating was almost done.

"What about that?" Kelly said, pointing to the Madonna picture leaning against the television cabinet.

"That goes on the wall. We need to take down that picture," Mrs. B said, pointing to a painting above the couch, "and put this up instead. I can't reach it. I'll have to ask somebody to hang it up."

"I can reach it. I can stand on the back of the couch." Kelly started to take off her shoes, and Mrs. B said, "No, Kelly. We need a grownup to do that."

Kelly thought for a minute. "Patrick's over the house with Julie. I'll go get him." She put her shoe back on and pulled on her coat.

Mrs. B started to say no and then thought, oh, for goodness sakes, what's the harm?

In a few minutes Patrick was there, taking down the faded farm scene and replacing it with the light-up Madonna.

"Will that reach to the extension cord?" Mrs. B asked from the corner where it was plugged.

Patrick handed her the cord and she stretched the extension. She plugged it in and the picture took on a golden glow.

"It looks beautiful!" Kelly said.

"Thank you, Patrick," Mrs. B said. "I appreciate your coming over." Mrs. B looked at Kelly.

"Yeah, thanks, Patrick," Kelly said.

"Sure, no problem." Patrick started to put on his Steeler jacket. "Hey, what happened the other night when Ron Monaghan was at your house? Was there some kind of emergency?"

"What do you mean?" Mrs. B asked, thoroughly confused.

"He was on your porch about two in the morning. At least I think it was him. I was driving home from Julie's. It looked like he was knocking on your door."

Mrs. B said, "I don't have any idea. If he knocked I didn't hear him. When was this?"

"I don't know, a week or so ago? It was a Friday night, I remember. Julie's dad let me stay late to watch a movie."

"I haven't a clue," Mrs. B said.

Patrick laughed. "Maybe he got loaded and went to the wrong house. My brother did that once."

Friday night. She gave him a half-hearted smile but her mind was elsewhere. The "leave it alone" note had come in Saturday's mail.

"Thanks again, Patrick," she said as she opened the door for him.

"Sure, Mrs. B."

As soon as he had gone, Kelly said, "Can we turn out the lights and sit in the dark with the Christmas lights on?"

"It's not dark outside yet," Mrs. B said, though it was getting toward dusk.

"Pleeeeeease?" Kelly asked.

"Okay, but only if we can be quiet for ten minutes. We'll sit in the dark and enjoy the lights. Is it a deal?" Mrs. B needed to think.

"Yeah. Do you want me to shut them off?" Kelly took off her shoes again and stood on the couch to reach the switch.

"Okay. Ten minutes, now. No talking."

"I promise." Kelly flipped the switch and sat on the couch, looking back and forth at the multicolored lights on the ceramic tree and the warm golden glow from the picture above her.

Mrs. B sat in her rocker, thinking. None of this made any sense. Why would Ron send those threatening notes? If he didn't steal the money, Mrs. B might find out who did. And if he did steal the money, Mrs. B might be able to find something to create a case for reasonable doubt. Either way Ron came out ahead. He had nothing to gain by trying to scare her off. And everything to lose.

And what about Father Clancy? Why would he lie to Myrtle about the cashier's check? Even if he was trying to make Myrtle feel better, it was cruel rather than kind to keep the truth from her. Father ought to know better.

Mrs. B sat quietly for a few minutes, looking at the lights. Then a decision came, like a bolt out of the blue.

She had to talk to Father Clancy. If Father walked her through the whole thing, step by step, from the very beginning, between the two of them they might be able to figure out when and how the money disappeared. And if Father did lie to Myrtle, Mrs. B needed to know why.

She'd never know if she didn't ask. It was as simple as that.

Just as she came to that realization, Kelly said, "Is it ten minutes yet?"

43

Mrs. B stood outside the little building attached to the rectory. The sign above the doorbell said, "Please ring and enter." She reached toward the bell, then put her hand back in her pocket and looked around.

It was late afternoon and everyone had gone home from the Senior Center. There was no one in the parking lot. Mrs. B lifted her hand again, and this time her finger pushed the little white button.

She walked inside and wiped her feet on the long industrial mat at the entrance. It was wet out, one of those unseasonable rains that come in the middle of winter. The temperature was in the fifties, but it was hard to enjoy it when it rained every hour or two.

There was a door to her right, open to an empty office. To her left was a desk that probably held a receptionist on busier days. Mrs. B realized she hadn't been in this building in years.

It looked pretty much the same as it always had. Maybe a new coat of paint.

Straight ahead was a white hallway. Father Clancy was standing in a doorway at the far end of the hall. He smiled and waved her toward him.

"Mrs. B. Come on in." As she walked down the hall she noticed the other doors in the small building were all shut. The place seemed deserted except for the two of them.

"I don't know whether it's nice or miserable out," Father said, taking her umbrella. She stuffed her gloves into a pocket, and he took her coat and hung it on a peg near the door.

Mrs. B didn't know what to say yet, so she didn't say anything. She had rehearsed how she would approach the subject, but it was all escaping her now.

Father motioned for her to sit. She took a green wing-backed chair and he took another. There was a small round table between them. Father said, "Can I get you a cup of coffee? I just drank the end of the old pot but it would only take a minute to make a new one."

"Thank you, Father, I'm fine." Mrs. B felt awkward and embarrassed. People visit their pastor to make arrangements for a christening, or to talk about a marital problem or a wayward child. Not to butt into church business. Not to say, "Father, I think I've caught you in a lie." She had a strong urge to make an excuse and leave, and it took all her willpower to stay in her seat.

Father Clancy leaned toward Mrs. B. "Well," he said. "How can I help you?"

He was still smiling, but now she wondered if he was putting on an act. Maybe she was too caught up in her thoughts to notice before.

She blurted out, "Father, I have something important to ask you. It's about Ronnie Monaghan."

Father sat back in his chair. His face turned soft and red at the same time. "I knew that's why you were here. I knew it. I knew it would happen one of these days. It had to happen. Oh, I don't know how I let Ron talk me into this." The old priest began to cry.

Mrs. B stared at him.

When the tears turned into sniffles, Mrs. B noticed a box of tissues on the table between them. She slid it toward him.

Father took a handful of tissues, one after the other, then blew his nose loudly. "I'm sorry, Edwina, I'm sorry. I'm sorry to make such a display."

Mrs. B hadn't uttered a profane word in twenty years, but the first thing that came to her mind was—what the hell is going on here?

44

It was a few minutes before Father Clancy regained his composure. When he finally began to talk, his speech was disjointed, like he was trying to tell Mrs. B everything at once. She struggled to make sense of it all.

"I don't know when it got out of hand. I couldn't even say. I always just played one-one-one. For years I just played one-one-one.

"Then I hit that first time. It was electrical. Electrical. Like a bolt of lightning went straight to my heart.

"It wasn't the money," Father said. "It was the winning. It was the winning."

For goodness sakes, Mrs. B thought. Everyone knew Father Clancy played the number one-one-one. He always told everyone that was his Holy Trinity number. "Three but they're all number one," he used to say. What on earth did that have to do with anything?

Oh, no. She took a deep breath, hoping against hope she was wrong.

"After I won that first time, I knew I could win again. I knew it," Father said. "So I started to play a second number. My mother's birthday sometimes, or numbers from my license plate. I'd switch it up.

"I did that for a long time. Years. Almost forgot what it felt like to win. Then I hit again, and it was that same jolt. You know how you give up candy for Lent, and you haven't had any candy for weeks and weeks, and then on Easter you have that chocolate bunny in your hand and you're just getting ready to bite off its ear and your mouth is watering and you know it's going to be the best thing you ever tasted in your whole life? That's what it felt like, Edwina."

Edwina. He'd called her Edwina again. He hadn't called her by her first name since Albert died. Mrs. B wanted to put her hands over her ears, to walk away, but she was the one who had opened this floodgate. She braced herself to hear the rest.

"I started playing three numbers," Father was saying. "Sometimes four. Never more than half a dozen. I'd get this feeling about a certain number and I'd have to play it. It was like I couldn't not play it. I knew this was the number. I knew this time I would win.

"After I hit the third time—it wasn't even much. I hit it boxed and, you know, when the numbers aren't in order, it's just a little bit of money. But I was so excited I won. I started to put two bucks on a number after that. Sometimes three." His voice softened so she could hardly hear it. "Sometimes five, really."

After a few seconds, he gave her an earnest, intent look. "I always played my numbers over at the Grill. It wasn't like everybody in the parish saw me dropping twenties at the lottery machine in the Mini-Mart. The people who knew were the guys at the bar. They don't care. Everybody there plays numbers. It's the same as drinking beer. It doesn't mean anything."

Father Clancy took a deep breath. "I could afford it, Edwina, that's the thing. I could afford it. I get a nice salary. Even with a new car every couple years, I still have money in my pocket. Money for charity, too," he was quick to add. "I always gave to the church and I always gave to Catholic Charities.

"I had enough money," he insisted. "I could afford it." The wad of tissues was still in his hand. He looked at the wastebasket across the room, then shoved them into his pocket.

"Even the football games," he said. "Twenty dollars here or there was nothing to me. I didn't even miss it.

"It was so much fun, Edwina. That was the thing. Even if I lost, a football game's totally different when there's money riding on it. I would sit at the bar and hoot and holler with the guys."

He stopped and let out a deep breath from the bottom of his chest. Then he looked down at his hands. Mrs. B looked at them, too. They were shaking.

"I didn't want the damned computer." He looked up. "Excuse my language, Edwina. I didn't want it. I didn't want to learn how to use a computer. What do I need a computer for? But back in January the diocese decided we all had to go to computer classes."

Mrs. B was lost now. What happened to the numbers? Why were they talking about his computer?

Father Clancy said, "So I went to the darned class but I couldn't figure out what was going on. Patrick, Tony Cordonelli's son, came over to tutor me. He's a good teacher, don't you think? He'll make something of himself one day."

Mrs. B nodded out of ingrained politeness.

"I was all fingers and thumbs," Father said. "I couldn't wrap my head around software and websites and all that.

"Patrick told me it was because I didn't know why I wanted to use the computer. He asked me a lot of questions about things I liked, and I couldn't think of anything that had to do with computers. So we sat around and shot the breeze for a while, and I told him I won $50 off his Uncle Pat on the Steelers game.

"Patrick asked me if it was worth $50 to me to learn the computer. I said sure. I gave him $50 and he went over his dad's store and came back with a prepaid credit card for me. Then he opened up a gambling website."

Mrs. B noticed she was gripping the armchair. She wanted to get up and leave, but she knew she had to stay. She put her hands in her lap and listened.

"I learned how to bet on a football game. Patrick used that website to show me all kinds of computer things, how to use the mouse and how to enter your credit card to buy something. I really did start to understand about the computer, but the whole time he was teaching me, all I could think about was betting on that website.

"After Patrick left I placed a $10 bet. I wasn't even sure if I did it right, but it turned out I did. Turned out I was a quick learner." He laughed, but it sounded hollow and sad.

"For a couple weeks I only did what I always did, twenty here, fifty there. But I thought about it all the time. All the time, Edwina. All the time. I thought about it all the time.

"Then I decided I wasn't going to bet on the computer any more. But every time I decided, I was back again at my desk, staring at the website Patrick showed me.

"I used to tell myself I was trying to learn how to use that internet. You can bet on the draft picks, did you know that?"

Mrs. B shook her head. Father didn't seem to notice.

"I spent the whole entire day thinking about what to bet on. One time I got up in the middle of the night and came over here in my pajamas to put money on who was going to win on that show, you know the one, where they sing. It's like *Ted Mack's Amateur Hour*.

"Anyhow. You have to use those prepaid credit cards because it's illegal, gambling on the computer. Not real illegal, only a little bit illegal, like playing numbers with a bookie. So I kept buying those credit cards. I would get them downtown or somewhere when I went out. I didn't want to get them at Tony's because I was buying a lot of them. A lot of them. Too many. I knew it was too many. Then pretty soon . . .

"Pretty soon I didn't have any money anymore."

Tears were rolling down his cheeks again, and Father reached for the tissues. Then he stood up and walked out the door.

45

Was Father Clancy coming back? For lack of a better option, Mrs. B stayed in her chair. The old priest did return, carrying a paper cup from the water cooler. He sat back down in the green wing-backed chair, looked at the paper cup and then at Mrs. B.

"I'm sorry, can I get you a glass of water?"

"No, I'm fine," Mrs. B said. It was a bald-faced lie. She had seldom been this far from fine.

When Father went back to his story, his voice was calmer, almost matter-of-fact. "The first time I borrowed from the church, it wasn't any big deal. I paid the money back and nobody ever knew. I would have told them if they asked. I'm sure I would have. But nobody ever asked."

He paused. "Maybe I wouldn't have told them why, but I'd have admitted to the borrowing. I know I would have. I'd already begun to think of excuses, just in case. Maybe a convent needed a loan. I thought that sounded good. Or a friend's friend died and there was no money for funeral expenses.

"I was going to lie like that, Edwina. I did plan to lie. But I never had to do it. Nobody ever asked."

The little bit of compassion Mrs. B had felt for him was withering away. How *could* he? How *dare* he?

Father said, "Somebody from the board counts the collection money after Mass, and I have to give them the deposit slips after I take the cash to the bank. But nobody ever touches that money old Doc Harrigan left us. The board can't agree on what to do with it yet, and it's in a whole separate account. It just sits there, and nobody looks at the bank statements." He shook his head back and forth. "They don't even open the envelopes. They just sit in a drawer until tax time.

"So I thought maybe I'd borrow from Dr. Harrigan's money. It's in one of those money markets. Me and Ronnie are the signatories, you knew that."

Mrs. B nodded. Her back was stiff, and she was trying very hard to stay composed.

"I was sure I'd have it all paid back before the end of the year. Then when the board asked, I would give them one of my excuses to explain why I had to borrow the money. If it was all paid back, they wouldn't care. Why would they care?

"So one morning when I was paying some bills, I went into the file cabinet. There were these plastic cards in with the statements. They're for getting money out of the machine at the bank."

Mrs. B flashed back to the morning she saw Father at the ATM machine before morning Mass.

"There they were, sitting in a file folder, still stuck to the cardboard they came on. I took one and put it in my pocket, and the next morning I tried working the machine at the bank. It tells you what to do," he said. "It's easy to use. Did you ever try it?"

Mrs. B had a dozen emotions battling inside her. She said she hadn't.

Father said, "It's easier than you think. So I started doing that early in the morning when nobody was around. I'd get the cash in the morning and buy the prepaid credit cards in the afternoon. Anyhow, I was on a winning streak. I figured I'd win it back right away, and then that would be that. I would stop. But then I started losing, and betting more to make it up and losing that, and betting more and losing that.

"Maybe I should have taken out a loan. Why didn't I take out a loan?" His face got red and soft again. "I kept thinking I was going to win tomorrow. Tomorrow I'll have the money and this will all be over."

He shook his head. "Then the diocese sent somebody to look at the books. They do that every year, surprise a different parish with an audit. Keeps everyone honest. They do it all the time. They weren't expecting to find anything."

Father's eyes got so sad, he reminded Mrs. B of a puppy dog. "When I knew the day the auditor was coming, I went fishing up at Conneaut Lake. I found a peaceful spot and fished all day and pretended I didn't have to come back.

"I got home late that night, the night the auditor made the report, and I went right to bed. In the morning I had a message from the diocese. They wanted me to call them, it was important. There was another message right after that, from the police.

"I didn't know it made a difference which card I used," he said. "I didn't know it mattered that I was using the card with Ronnie's name on it. I thought they were both the same."

He stopped, then moved his head back and forth slowly, looking down at the floor. "Maybe that's not even true," he said. "Maybe I did know. Maybe I knew."

46

Father Clancy bent over and covered his face with his hands. His shoulders shook. Unconsciously, Mrs. B pushed the box of tissues in his direction again. He didn't seem to notice.

"The police wanted to talk to me before they arrested Ron. That's what their message was. I called Ron on his cell phone as soon as I heard the message," Father said between sobs. "Ron left work and came right over.

"I had to tell Ron before I confessed to the police. It was the right thing to do."

He sat up in his chair. "Ron told me I was an addict. He took me all the way out to Hopewood to a Gamblers Anonymous meeting. So I wouldn't run into anybody from the diocese.

"I go twice a week now. And I haven't placed one bet since then. Scared straight," he said before he blew his nose again. "Ron's been good to me. He knows a lot about addiction."

Mrs. B remembered a night, about a week before Leo and Ronnie left for California. Those two stumbled into her living room at three in the morning, high as kites, and broke her good lamp. Now Ron had that contracting business, and a wife and those sweet little boys. Ron must know something about addiction. He did turn himself around.

"Ron told me to stay away from the bar. He said I had to go once in a while so nobody wondered where I was and started putting two and two together. But he said I could only go when he could meet me there. So that's what I do.

"And I go twice a week to the Gamblers Anonymous meeting. And I call people there if I want to make a bet and if I wait it out, after a while, the feeling goes away. It's a nice drive out to Hopewood. Pretty scenery. You ever go out that way?"

Scenery! Mrs. B said she hadn't been there.

"Anyhow, this was all Ron's idea. He said I can't say anything yet. From the get-go, he was sure the diocese would close St. Mary's if they found out it was me. He'd been going to the diocesan meetings about the church closings, and they kept talking about fiscal leadership and all that sort of thing. So Ron said we had to stall until he could think of something. So you can't say anything about this, Edwina. We have to wait until Ron figures out what we need to do next."

Mrs. B was smack in the middle of this now. How could she agree to that? How could she not? Her stomach hurt.

"That story about the cashier's check, Ron thought that up. He said we needed to have a story ready so we could throw people off the track. I didn't want to lie to Myrtle Monaghan, but when she asked me I had to tell her something. So I told her Ron's story.

"The police didn't even ask me about the money, they were so sure it was Ron, because he had a record. They kept saying they couldn't understand why we'd give him access to the account. They acted like we were idiots."

Father's face got red again and his eyes filled with tears. "They were so sure it was Ron," he said again. "And Ron, he was willing to let himself get arrested so he could try to save St. Mary's. I told him it was noble. Wasn't that noble, Edwina? Wasn't that noble of him?"

It was noble. Mrs. B nodded.

"Ron shrugged it off. Said he wasn't afraid to sit in a jail cell for a few hours. 'It's not like I never did it before,' he said."

Father sat back in his chair. His hands were steadier and his face was returning to its natural color. "I'm glad you know now, Edwina. I'm glad someone else knows. It's been a burden, this whole thing. It's been a burden."

I would think so, Mrs. B thought.

Father bent toward her and looked straight into her eyes. "You can't say anything. Not yet. I promised Ron."

She didn't reply.

He leaned closer. His voice was stronger and more composed. "Ron's got a good head on his shoulders. He deals with these diocese people all the time. I promised I'd listen to him."

Mrs. B stared at the old priest. Compassion and anger battled inside her. She couldn't promise anything. She needed time to take this all in.

"Father, I can't talk about this right now," she said finally. She stood up, gathered her belongings and walked out the door.

47

At five thirty in the morning, Mrs. B gave up on sleeping and put on a pot of coffee.

She wasn't the kind of woman who lived a life full of moral dilemmas. Either something was right or it was wrong. It had been a long time since she'd had to face shades of gray.

On one hand, there was what should be her only choice. The truth is the truth. How many times had she told her kids they had to tell the truth? That telling the truth is the right thing, the only thing to do?

Ron and Father Clancy didn't have the right to keep the truth from the parish, from the police, from anybody. Neither did Mrs. B.

If she went to the police and told them the truth, Ron would go free, as he certainly should.

But . . .

What if he was right about the way the diocese would deal with it?

The church would close. Everyone in Burchfield would have to travel by bus or by car to go to Mass on Sunday. Many of her friends didn't have cars, and some couldn't even drive anymore. Some of her friends had trouble taking the bus on a nice day, let alone a snowy day or in 90-degree weather.

It was likely the Senior Center would shut down. Though that would be a terrible thing, it would be unfair to make it her main concern. She tried to shove that thought to the back of her mind.

What else?

There would be no more stopping in to the church to see a neighbor child's baptism or first communion or graduation.

Oh. Oh, my.

They could decide to close the school.

The public school was a fine school, but it wasn't Saint Mary's. If Mrs. B went to the police, one repercussion could be that a generation—no, future generations—would be denied a Catholic education.

It was a big responsibility, having this information.

Mrs. B hated it.

If Ron was right and Father Clancy was an addict . . . well, turning someone in to the police was not always the best way to deal with addiction. Mrs. B had a lot of respect for the police, but she knew from her experience with Leo that they weren't going to treat an addict with patience and understanding. That job was reserved for mothers.

There was no good way out of this.

Mrs. B noticed a pound of butter on the kitchen table and, without thinking, stood up to put it into the refrigerator where it belonged. Then she stopped in her tracks.

The butter was on the table because she had put it there to give it time to soften. Today was the day she and Myrtle were staying home from the Senior Center to bake Christmas cookies. She was expected at Myrtle's at nine.

As much as Mrs. B enjoyed her company, Myrtle was the last person she wanted to see right now.

Pouring herself another cup of coffee, Mrs. B spent the next two hours going over her dilemma, weighing consequences both to her parish and to her soul.

At a quarter to eight, she gave it up. The truth had been secret for quite a while. One more day wasn't going to make a difference. She got dressed, worked a little on the crossword and began to gather the things she wanted to take to Myrtle's house.

48

When Mrs. B got to Myrtle's, she was surprised to see Ron in the front yard setting up a ladder. Next to him was a jumbled mass of Christmas lights.

"Better late than never. Right, Mrs. B?" he said as she approached. He walked toward her and met her on the sidewalk, stealing a quick glance toward the front door. Taking the canvas bag she was carrying, he bent over and said quietly, "Father Clancy called me last night."

Mrs. B was surprised that a grown man could look so much like a little boy.

"Are you going to tell Mom?" Ron asked.

"I'm not going to say anything to anyone today," Mrs. B said.

"Thank you," Ron said. His relief was palpable.

Mrs. B didn't want to give the wrong impression. "When tomorrow comes, I'll decide what to do. I just came here to bake Christmas cookies."

Just then, Myrtle came to the door and waved to Mrs. B through the window. Ron carried the canvas bag inside and Mrs. B followed him. She took off her jacket and tossed it onto the arm of Myrtle's couch. "It's nice in here," she said.

"I just turned the oven on," Myrtle said.

The kitchen smelled like lemon. The counter was wet, and Mrs. B saw a sponge and a bottle of lemon dish soap at the sink. A little white radio was playing Christmas carols. The table was covered with colorful plastic bowls and measuring cups and little sparkly bottles of red and green sugar. Towering over it all was a large canister that said "Flour" in big gold letters.

Ron said, "Mom, I got to head out to the job site for a couple hours. I'll be back."

"I thought you wanted to hang the lights," Myrtle said.

"I will. I'll come back in a few hours. I just got to check on the guys, see if they need anything."

"Well, move the ladder over to the end of the porch. I don't want it in the way when the mailman comes."

He bent down and kissed her. "I will. I'll be back in a couple hours. You better have some cookies waiting for me."

"You can't eat too many!" she called toward the front door as he was leaving. "These are for Christmas."

Myrtle turned back to Mrs. B. "I told Ronnie he didn't have to hang the Christmas lights, and he wasn't going to, and then this morning when I was getting ready for you to come over he said he was going to stay home and hang them up. I told him he didn't have to, but I do like the lights. I wish everybody's house had lights for Christmas. Did you bring vanilla?"

Mrs. B emptied the contents of her bag into the jumble on the table. A flowered apron, two cookie sheets, nutmeg, butter, poppy seeds, powdered sugar, chocolate chips, vanilla. At the very bottom was a sandwich bag full of index cards. "I brought my chocolate chip recipe, and my gingerbread recipe," Mrs. B said, shuffling through them as she talked. "And the one for poppy seed cake."

"Ooh, I'm glad you brought real butter. Sometimes you tell people butter and they bring you oleo."

"I knew you wanted to make shortbread. Butter's always better for shortbread." Mrs. B was still looking at the recipes.

Myrtle washed her hands at the sink, then wiped them on a dishtowel. "Do you think we should make the gingerbread? I thought we should but now I don't know. The kids never eat it."

Mrs. B considered. "You're probably right. You and I would eat it and we don't need the extra calories."

"Where do you want to start?" Myrtle said, clearing a space at the end of the table.

"Let's do the shortbread first," Mrs. B said, tying on her apron. "Then they can cool while we're making the chocolate chips."

"I have my Christmas tree and my star," Myrtle said proudly as she held the cookie cutters aloft. "The dough sticks in the stars and you have to push it some, but they look so pretty when they're done."

Myrtle measured butter and powdered sugar into a yellow bowl and started to cream them together with a wooden spoon. Mrs. B placed two cookie sheets on top of the stove, poured a little oil on them and rubbed it around with a piece of waxed paper. Bing Crosby started to croon "I'm Dreaming of a White Christmas," and the ladies sang along while they worked.

The first batch of shortbread was a little burnt around the edges, but the rest were fine. They put them aside to cool and started on the chocolate chips.

At lunchtime Myrtle made chipped ham sandwiches with yellow mustard. The two women ate them in the living room while they watched the noon news.

By three thirty that afternoon, they had six plates of chocolate chips and ten plates of shortbread cookies—red stars with green sparkles, and green trees with red sparkles. When they were starting on the poppy seed cake, they could hear Ron on the porch, putting up the ladder again.

Myrtle looked around the kitchen. "With half these cookies and half the cake you'll have lots to feed your company. Are they coming Christmas Eve or Christmas Day?"

"They're coming at noon on Christmas," Mrs. B said, flouring a bundt pan. "I'm going to early Mass Christmas Eve so I have all morning to cook."

"Early Mass Christmas Eve is the best one," Myrtle said. "I like the children's choir. I don't think they should have Santa at the Mass, though. I don't think that's right."

"I don't know whose idea that was last year. I didn't like it either," Mrs. B said.

When the cake was in the oven, they cleaned the kitchen as best they could with all the clutter, then Myrtle wiped her hands on her apron. "We still have almost an hour till that's done. Let's go watch TV."

They went into the living room and tuned in to the tail end of a sitcom. After the advertisements, *It's A Wonderful Life* began.

"I just watched this the other day," Mrs. B said.

"Want me to change the channel?" Myrtle said.

"No, please don't. I love this movie."

"Me, too. It's so Christmasy," Myrtle said. "I didn't get to see it yet this year. So far I just saw *Holiday Inn*."

"I like *White Christmas* better," Mrs. B said.

"Me too," Myrtle said. They both settled in on the couch, still in their aprons. They sat like that for almost an hour. Mrs. B didn't fall asleep, but she thought about it.

During an advertisement, Myrtle went to the kitchen to check on the cake. Mrs. B was leaning back on the couch, still thinking about the movie. She had a warm feeling remembering Kelly's sleepy face as she assured the child that everything had turned out fine. The nice rich guy saved the day and everyone sang a song at the end.

Mrs. B bolted upright and pulled on her coat. She stuck her head through the kitchen doorway. "I'm going outside for a second."

"Tell Ronnie I'm making a pot of coffee if he wants some," Myrtle said. "I'll give him those burnt cookies. He won't care."

Mrs. B pulled the front door shut and walked into the yard. She stood at the bottom of the ladder, hands in her pockets, and looked up. "Ron, can I talk to you a minute?"

49

Mrs. B finally found the toothpicks in the cupboard above the sink, behind a bag of sugar.

The ham was in a roasting pan on the kitchen table, already covered with cloves and pineapple. She opened a jar of maraschino cherries and popped one in her mouth, then stuck a toothpick through another and placed it carefully in the center of a pineapple ring.

When the ham was fully decorated, she covered it with her special glaze of ginger ale and brown sugar, then put it in the oven and looked at the clock.

The morning went by quickly. She finished the quick crossword and attempted the Chicago one, but she kept remembering one more thing she wanted to get ready and soon gave it up altogether.

Twice she thought about her conversation with Ron, and twice she pushed it from her mind. Today was Christmas, and she had company coming.

The smell of ham filled the kitchen. When it was almost done, she opened a can of sweet potatoes, dumped them in a pot with some orange juice and a handful of raisins, and turned the fire on low. She pulled out a cookie sheet for the rolls, placed it next to the sweet potatoes, then took the ham out of the oven and set it on a platter to cool.

She pulled carrots and celery out of the vegetable bin in the refrigerator, then cut them into sticks and arranged them on a plate. When she opened the refrigerator to make room for the plate, she ran across a block of cream cheese, so she went back and stuffed the celery sticks and sprinkled them with paprika. Then she cleared the kitchen table.

The Christmas tablecloth was sitting on the corner of her bedroom dresser. It was white, with red candy canes, and looked almost new. She spread it carefully, then wiped the vinyl with a damp dishcloth. After the table was set, she went into the living room to turn on the Christmas lights. A few minutes later she found herself back in her bedroom, looking for a ceramic Santa to put on the kitchen table.

At noon, she looked out the front door window. The street was quiet. She left the door slightly ajar and went back to start the crescent rolls. Just as she put them in the oven, Kelly came into the kitchen, her mother trailing behind her.

"Merry Christmas!" The little girl was dressed in a red sweatshirt and red pants. She was all smiles.

"We knocked but then Kelly came right in. I hope that's alright," Michele said.

"That's why I left the door open. Merry Christmas," Mrs. B said, taking off her apron.

"I brought you a present," Kelly said. "Come open it. It's in the living room."

"Mrs. B's busy right now," Michele said.

"It's fine," Mrs. B said. "Everything's done. We just need to wait for the rolls. You have a watch on, Michele. Tell me when it's ten minutes."

Michele glanced at the time. Mrs. B shut off the sweet potatoes and put a lid on the pot. Then she bent down and said to Kelly, "Let's go open presents."

In the living room, Michele took off her coat and put it on the arm of the couch. Mrs. B reached underneath the table near her rocker and pulled out two packages, both wrapped in green paper covered with tiny brown reindeer and tiny red sleighs.

"Here," Kelly said, thrusting a small box toward Mrs. B. Its white and gold wrapping glittered in the light.

"Kelly, wait. Let Mrs. B sit down," Michele said.

Mrs. B handed Michele the gifts she was holding and then sat. Kelly stood so close to her chair that Mrs. B had to be careful not to rock on her toes. She unwrapped the box, trying not to tear the pretty wrapping, and unfolded the tissue paper inside.

"It's a potholder!" Kelly said triumphantly. "I made it!"

"She really did," Michele said. "She made me take her to the craft store."

It was woven together with cotton loops of pink and purple. Mrs. B took it out and held it in both hands. She was surprised to feel her eyes well up with tears, and had to take a deep breath before she could say, "Why, thank you, Kelly. It's beautiful."

"I can make you another one but it'll have to be a different color. I don't have any more purple," Kelly said.

Mrs. B was still looking at the potholder. Michele held up a package and said, "Kelly, this big one is for you from Mrs. B."

Kelly came running over to open it. She tore the paper and threw it on the floor, then looked at her mother and picked it back up again.

"*Scholastic Children's Encyclopedia*," Michele read from the cover.

Kelly opened it and began to look at the pictures. Michele asked her daughter, "What do you say?"

Kelly went over and gave Mrs. B a big hug. "Thanks, Mrs. B!"

Michele said, "It's almost time. Do you want me to check on the rolls?"

"Please," Mrs. B said. Kelly was kneeling on the floor. She had the book on the seat of the couch while she paged through it.

"Kelly, come on. It's time to eat," Mrs. B said as she rose from her chair. Kelly stood up, still looking at the book.

"Come on. Your mother's waiting for us," Mrs. B said and walked toward the kitchen. The little girl followed.

Michele started to take a seat at the kitchen table when Kelly said, "No, Mom, that's my chair. You sit here." Michele caught Mrs. B's eye and the two of them exchanged a grin as Michele obediently changed places.

Mrs. B was pulling the plate full of carrots and celery from the refrigerator. "Michele, there's a bottle of ginger ale in here. Would you mind pouring everyone a glass?"

Michele poured three glasses, Kelly's halfway.

Kelly tasted it. "Eww," she said. Michele began to reprimand her but Mrs. B was already at her chair, filling the rest of the glass with orange juice.

"Better now?" Mrs. B said.

Kelly tasted it. "Yes," she said.

"Well, let's fill our plates. We're doing buffet style today," Mrs. B said. Michele reached for her plate.

"What's that mean?" Kelly said.

"It means come over here with your plate and get your own food," Michele said.

Mrs. B put ham and sweet potatoes on Kelly's plate, then added a crescent roll. "I can eat two of those," Kelly said.

"When you eat that one, you can have as many more as you want," Mrs. B said.

Michele had taken ham and rolls, and was hovering over the sweet potatoes. Kelly said, "Take some, Mom. She doesn't make you eat it if you don't like it." Michele stirred the pot, then took a spoonful.

Mrs. B made herself a plate, and they all sat down to eat.

50

After dinner, Mrs. B settled into her rocker. Though exhaustion was starting to creep in, she absolutely refused to acknowledge it. She was enjoying her guests.

Just as she was reaching for a cookie from a tray on the coffee table, Michele handed her a long flat box with glittery wrapping. "Here, Mrs. B. I got you this."

Mrs. B put the cookie back down. "Oh goodness, we didn't exchange gifts yet! I have something for you, too."

"You gave me it already. I have it right here," Michele said, reaching for the gift covered in green-

and-red reindeer paper. She set it in her lap while Mrs. B opened Michele's shiny package.

Inside the box was a large square scarf. A floral pattern covered its powder blue background. "It's so silky!" Mrs. B said as she folded it into a triangle and draped it over her shoulders. "This will match my coat perfectly."

Michele's gift was a tin of lavender and ginger tea. She read the sides of the canister, then lifted the lid and smelled it. "Ooh!" she said. "Mind if I make some?"

"Go right ahead. There's a little pot on the shelf by the stove."

"Would you like a cup?" Michele asked.

"No, but when you come back would you mind pouring me some coffee? With a little bit of milk?"

As Michele headed toward the kitchen, Kelly piped up. "Mom. Mom!"

Michele came back and stuck her head in the living room doorway. "What?"

Kelly looked up from the encyclopedia. "What do you think is the fastest animal?"

"I don't know, a greyhound?"

"Nope, a cheetah." Kelly gave her a superior look that almost made Mrs. B laugh out loud.

Michele called out a minute later from the kitchen. "Mrs. B, where's the sugar?"

"Go tell your mom it's on the shelf above the sink," Mrs. B said to Kelly.

Kelly hollered, "It's on the shelf above the sink!"

Mrs. B laughed despite herself. "That's not what I meant."

Kelly, oblivious, stuck a finger in the book to mark her page and went to the coffee table for a red star cookie. She handed Mrs. B a green tree cookie, then sat back on the loveseat with the book in her lap.

Michele came into the living room and handed Mrs. B her coffee, then settled into the barcalounger with a cup of tea and two chocolate chip cookies. Mrs. B decided she'd been too quick to judge Michele. The young woman must struggle as a single mom, and she'd been nothing but lovely today.

They sat in silence for a few minutes, then Kelly looked up from her book. "Can we turn on the TV?"

"Sure," Mrs. B said. "See if there's a good movie on." She put her feet up on her footstool. Kelly flipped through the channels until she found *A Christmas Story*.

"Oh, good, it's just starting," Michele said.

Mrs. B had never seen the movie before but Michele and Kelly seemed to know it scene by scene. Kelly got a big kick out of the youngest brother's antics, and Mrs. B had fun watching Kelly giggle.

Her neighbors left before the movie was over. "We've seen it a million times," Michele said as Mrs. B let them out the front door. Kelly was carrying her book. Michele had the tin of tea in one hand and a package of ham wrapped in aluminum foil in the other.

"Thanks again, Mrs. B," Michele said.

"You can have sandwiches for lunch tomorrow," Mrs. B said.

"Mom! Can we buy raisin bread?" Kelly said, already halfway down the steps. Michele ignored her and, as she shut the door, Mrs. B could hear Kelly asking again.

Mrs. B watched them cross the street, then settled into her rocker until the movie ended. When it was over, she put away the rest of the cookies and cleaned the kitchen. Then she stretched out on the couch and covered herself with an afghan. For a moment her eyes opened with worry, but she chided herself. The situation was in Ron's hands now. She'd done everything she could, and it did no one any good for her to lie here and think about it. She closed her eyes, took a deep breath and fell into a nice long nap.

51

Helen called a little before six o'clock. Eleven o'clock London time.

"Merry Christmas, Mom!"

"Merry Christmas, honey," Mrs. B said. It was good to hear her daughter's voice. "What did you do today?"

"I had to work in the morning, but only for a little while," Helen said. "The office was full of cakes and cupcakes, everyone trying to make up for the fact they were working on Christmas, I suppose. Then Malcolm and I exchanged gifts and had some French toast, and afterward we went over to his parents for dinner. I feel like all I did today was eat! How about you? How was your Christmas?"

Mrs. B realized how much she had enjoyed her day. She tried not to sound too happy so Helen wouldn't feel left out. "The new neighbors came over, the ones I told you about."

"With the little girl?"

"Kelly. Yes. They ate here and then we watched a movie. We had a nice time."

"Oh, that's good." Mrs. B could hear relief in Helen's voice.

"Do you want to open gifts now?" Mrs. B asked.

"Sure. You can go first," Helen said.

"No, you go first, honey."

Helen opened the decorating book and made a suitable fuss over it. Mrs. B's gift, inside the shipping box, was wrapped in blue and silver paper. As she pulled it out, the package bent. Maybe a magazine? She opened it.

"*The Guardian Weekly*," Mrs. B read from the masthead.

"I got you a subscription," Helen said. "People here say it's the most balanced news reporting in the world. I know how you hate journalists who editorialize."

Mrs. B was already paging through the newspaper. "A real journalist doesn't editorialize," she said.

"That's the definition of journalism." She thanked her daughter. "Honey, this was a really thoughtful gift."

"Oh, you're welcome, Mom. I'm glad you like it." Helen sounded like she'd just been congratulated on a straight-A report card.

After they said their goodbyes, Mrs. B leafed through *The Guardian Weekly* to see if there was a crossword puzzle. There was, on the second to last page. She folded it over and picked up a pencil, then sat for quite a while reading first one clue, then another. It looked like this one might take her all week.

52

A few days later, Mrs. B had just eaten her last spoonful of bean and sauerkraut soup when she heard a knock at the kitchen door. She put the bowl in the sink and through the door's little window saw a blue and orange Chicago Bears jacket on what looked like a very large man. Then there was Danny McCoy, waving.

Mrs. B opened the door. "Mrs. B!" He picked her up and gave her a great big hug. Ron Monaghan stood next to him in the doorway. The room felt suddenly charged with energy, like a long-ago summer day after a Little League game.

"Come on in, both of you, and shut the door," Mrs. B said. "We'll all catch our death of cold." She turned to Danny. "Now shouldn't you be in Chicago? Don't the Bears have a game in a couple of days?"

"Late Christmas with the folks. I'm flying out tonight," Danny said.

The two men sat at the kitchen table. Mrs. B went to the sink to start a fresh pot of coffee.

"Boy, this is just like old times, isn't it, Danny?" Ron said.

"Yeah, do you have any cheese and crackers?" Danny said. The two men laughed.

"If you're hungry, everything's in the same place it always was. I never knew you to be shy before." She reached above the sink for a bowl of sugar and put it on the table, then went to the china hutch for two coffee mugs and a couple of spoons.

"We're not hungry," Ron said. "Mrs. McCoy made us ham sandwiches. I just don't remember us ever sitting at this table without cheese and crackers."

"Well, you're grown men now," Mrs. B said. "You can have coffee."

Danny was looking all around the room, taking everything in. "I feel like a little kid again, Mrs. B." Mrs. B looked around, too, and realized not much had changed in her kitchen over the years. New refrigerator and stove, but they were in the same place as the old ones. Different linoleum floor.

They all got quiet for a few seconds. Mrs. B knew everyone was thinking about Leo, though no one said his name. She broke the silence. "How about some cookies?"

The excitement returned. Danny said, "Sure, I could go for a cookie. How about you, Ron?"

Mrs. B opened a clear container filled to the brim with alternating layers of shortbread and wax paper. She moved her newspaper out of the way and put the plastic bin on the table. "Help yourselves, boys." They both reached in while she filled their mugs with coffee.

Danny stirred in some sugar. "There was another reason I came home. I had an appointment down at the diocesan office," he said.

Oh! Despite herself, Mrs. B could feel her legs getting weak. She pulled out a chair and sat down.

Danny paused for a moment, then broke out in a big smile. "Your plan worked like a charm."

Mrs. B's hand went to her heart. "Oh, thank goodness. Thank goodness."

"You were right," Danny said as he took a sip of coffee. "All they cared about was the money. As soon as I made the donation to St. Mary's, they dropped the charges against Ronnie. Told the police it was all a big mistake." He added a little more sugar and gave the mug a stir. "Of course, I made a nice donation to the diocese, too."

"Nobody knows about Father Clancy?" Mrs. B said.

Danny put his mug down on the table with a satisfied thud. "No one even mentioned his name."

"Oh, that's wonderful," Mrs. B said. She reached for a cookie.

"I gave them a promissory note. The check will come later, from my lawyer." Danny had a twinkle in his eye. "I'm adding a stipulation. The money stays at St. Mary's. If the money's still there and the church closes, the entire amount goes to the Catholic Youth Organization to pay for athletic equipment."

Ron brushed crumbs off the front of his shirt. "The diocese can never get their hands on it," he said.

Mrs. B thought about this for a minute. "Does Father know yet?"

"We told him last night. We met him down the Grill," Ron said.

Danny laughed. "I told him he has to pay me back, every penny. He promised to send me $250 a month." Mrs. B started to mentally do the math when Ron interrupted her.

"Mrs. B, thank you for everything. I mean it. And I want to apologize for those notes I left in your mailbox. I hope you weren't too scared," he said.

Mrs. B looked up from her coffee. "I wasn't scared."

"See, I told you, Ron," Danny said, biting into another cookie.

53

Mass was at four thirty and confession was at three. Mrs. B left the house at two thirty. She wanted time to say some prayers for Leo before everyone got there. It would be her Christmas present to her son.

When she got to St. Mary's, Father Clancy was just unlocking the door. As she stepped into the vestibule he took both her hands in his.

"Thank you, Mrs. B. Thank you. I'm going to pay Danny back," he said earnestly. "Every single penny, if it takes me all my life."

Part of her knew he was an addict but another part didn't want to let him off the hook. "It'll take you longer than that," Mrs. B said.

Father looked at her quizzically.

"Two hundred and fifty dollars a month for ten years is $30,000. How much was gone from that account?"

He dropped her hands. "Oh," he said, crestfallen. "I didn't think of that."

A glimpse of light came into the far end of the church, and they both turned toward it. Rose was walking through the back door to set up the altar linens. She spotted Mrs. B at the far end of the long aisle and waved.

Mrs. B waved back, then turned to Father and whispered, "You know, I even suspected Rose of taking that money."

"Rose?" Father said. "Why on earth Rose?"

Mrs. B felt sheepish now that she'd said it. "It was silly, really. It was because none of us knows anything about her. It's like her life started when she got married and moved to Burchfield."

Father Clancy looked around, even though there were only the two of them in the vestibule. He lowered his voice. "Rose is embarrassed about the way she met her husband. I told her she shouldn't be embarrassed, nobody cares about that sort of thing anymore, but she doesn't like to talk about it."

Mrs. B didn't want to pry into something her friend obviously wanted to be kept private, but before she could stop him, Father went on.

"When Rose was a young girl, a teenager really, she got a job as a hoochie-coochie dancer down at one of those clubs on Liberty Avenue. Her very first night the place was raided. Poor thing was scared to death. Her Bob was a rookie cop on the raid. When he saw the look on her face he hurried up and hid her in a cupboard. She stayed there and he came back to get her after everyone was gone. Cupid's dart," Father finished with a wink.

Mrs. B looked down the aisle at Rose, who was smoothing a white linen onto the altar. Wow, she thought. It was amazing how much a person could change. It gave her hope for Leo.

Leo. She came to church early to pray for Leo. She turned to Father to make her excuses and found him looking at his watch.

"I still have time," he muttered to himself, then turned to Mrs. B. "I'm saying Mass, and Father Sean's doing the confessions. If you see him tell him I went over the Grill to look for Lefty Cameron."

Confession. Mrs. B had to go to confession, too. She made her way down the aisle and took a pew near the front.

54

Mrs. B had just folded the pretty blue babushka Michele gave her and put it in her pocket when Father Sean arrived. She relayed the message that Father Clancy would be back soon. The young priest looked down at his watch. Then he looked up at Mrs. B and smiled.

He reminded her of someone. For the first time she really looked at his face.

As he turned and went into the confessional, she realized that young Father Sean looked like Artie Fleming, the boy who sat behind her in grade school who used to pull her hair. Though it had never occurred to her before, she realized Artie was probably trying to get her attention. He might have even had a crush on her.

Father Sean was a perfectly nice young man.

She gave him some time to get settled, then entered the confessional and knelt down. "Bless me, Father, for I have sinned."

"How long has it been since your last confession?" Father Sean asked.

"Oh, I don't know," Mrs. B said. "Not that long."

"Okay," Father said. "What are your sins, my child?"

Mrs. B did like the "my child." Very old-fashioned. Must be the Irish influence.

"I committed a sin of omission, Father. And I have been quick to judge."

55

People began to filter in at around a quarter to four, and Mass started right on time. When Father Clancy stepped up to the pulpit for the announcements, he looked happier than Mrs. B had seen him in a long, long while.

"I'm overjoyed to tell you the diocese has decided St. Mary's will stay open." The news was met with spontaneous applause, followed by a quiet murmur while parishioners shared their relief.

Father waited for the congregation to settle down. "The diocese does still plan to close five churches, but St. Mary's has been removed from their list. It is a time of rejoicing for all of us.

"Our reading from Luke today is full of joy and promise. A new year is upon us. Our Lord promises us so much. But what do we promise Him?" Mrs. B sat back, pleased and satisfied, to listen to the homily.

Mrs. B stayed in her pew after Mass until the church was almost empty. When she finally rose, Father Clancy was still at the front door, greeting the last few parishioners as they left.

Mrs. B was the first one in today and the last one out. She felt a little pride at the distinction.

When she reached the doorway, Father Clancy reached out to shake her hand, then leaned over and said, "Lefty's going to write me up a nice insurance policy, with Danny McCoy as beneficiary. I told him, 'Lefty, I hope to live a good long life but I'll never outlive that young man. He's done a lot for St. Mary's. He'll do something good with that money.'"

Well, well, that was quick thinking on Father Clancy's part. Mrs. B had always seen him as a loving, caring pastor, but she never thought he was the brightest bulb in the box. It made her wonder now if she'd underestimated him all these years. Quick to judge again, she chided herself.

As she reached the bottom of the church steps, she saw Myrtle standing on the sidewalk. Mrs. B waved. Her friend ran over, threw her arms around her and gave Mrs. B a big, loud kiss on the cheek.

"I thanked the Blessed Mother, too," Myrtle said, grinning from ear to ear.

As the two women linked arms and walked toward the corner, they heard Don call out, "Wish us a happy anniversary, ladies!" There he was at the end of the parking lot, wearing a snappy fedora instead of his usual ball cap. Will wonders never cease.

He was opening the car door for his wife. "Can we give you a lift?" Don asked.

Myrtle shook her head and Mrs. B said, "Oh, no, we can walk. How many years?"

"What?" Don said.

"Forty-five. Forty-five years we've been married," Mary Ann said just before he shut her door.

Forty-five. That gave him five more years to figure out how to get her to Paris.

56

When she got home, Mrs. B was surprised to find Kelly on her front porch.

"Kelly, what are you doing here?"

The child was sitting on the glider, a box in her lap. "Aunt Laverne sent me this game in the mail but I don't know how to play it."

"Does your mother know you're here?" Mrs. B glanced over at their house. The lights were on in the living room.

Kelly looked over there, too. "Yeah, she's got a new boyfriend. They're watching some stupid thing on TV." She turned back to Mrs. B and said defiantly, "Nobody wanted to play with me."

Mrs. B looked at Michele's house again. So much for being too quick to judge. She put her key in the lock and opened her front door.

"Come on in, honey. Let's figure out how to play that game." Kelly trotted ahead and Mrs. B watched the hood of her pink sweatshirt bob up and down over the back of her little winter coat. As they walked toward the kitchen, Mrs. B put her arm around Kelly's shoulder. "I have some of those Christmas cookies left," she said. "Which would you like, a green tree or a red star?"

Kelly looked up at Mrs. B, a smile lighting her tiny face. "A red star. Can I have milk, too?"

"You certainly can," said Mrs. B.